# -A NEW HERO-

CURTIS JOBLING

PUFFIN

PUFFIN BOOKS

UK | USA | Canada | Ireland | Australia
India | New Zealand | South Africa

Puffin Books is part of the Penguin Random House group of companies
whose addresses can be found at global.penguinrandomhouse.com.

puffinbooks.com

First published 2015
001

Written by Curtis Jobling
Copyright © Mind Candy Ltd, 2015

World of Warriors and all related elements ™ and
copyright © Mind Candy Ltd, 2015
All rights reserved

The moral right of the author has been asserted

Set in 12/16 pt Baskerville and 10/16 pt Raleway
Typeset by Jouve (UK), Milton Keynes
Printed in Great Britain by Clays Ltd, St Ives plc

A CIP catalogue record for this book is available from the British Library

ISBN: 978-0-141-36002-7

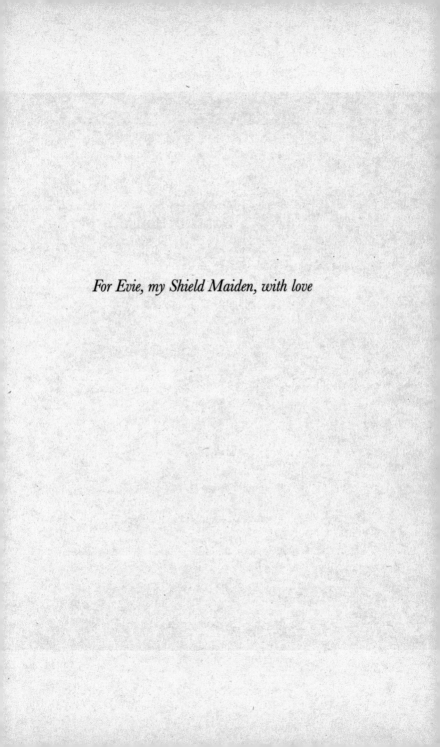

*For Evie, my Shield Maiden, with love*

# CHAPTER ONE

'Get a blooming move on!'

Dad's voice echoed round the tiny flat, sending shockwaves resonating through Trick Hope's body. The thirteen-year-old lay for a moment longer, thinking about the day ahead, before swinging his legs out from beneath the covers. He shambled to his feet, scratched and stretched. Hooking the vertical blinds aside, he peered out of the window. London sprawled before him.

Trick lifted the lucky pendant round his neck to his lips, giving it a swift ritual kiss before letting it fall back on to his chest. He sifted through the clothes on his bedroom floor for his school shirt and drainpipes. After squeezing into the jeans, he tugged on the shirt – still buttoned from the night before – and slipped the knotted tie over his head like a noose.

He stepped into his once-white trainers, then he

walked over to the shelves beside the door. They were loaded with his comic collection, weeklies bought religiously from Super Freaks in Soho.

Trick wasn't looking at the comics, though. His focus was on the terrarium nestled between the piles of back issues. There was no movement within the glass tank; the foliage and webs were motionless. Shelob had clearly been hungry in the night, polishing off the last of her crickets.

'You'll be late!'

Trick rolled his eyes, making no attempt to quicken his pace. He shrugged his blazer on, the maroon sleeves threadbare from the various scrapes he'd got himself into over the years. Lifting the flap on his backpack, he checked the contents: a half-empty box of Tic Tacs, a tatty exercise book and a couple of biros. Hardly the ingredients for academic success. Trick shrugged. What had school ever really taught him, apart from how to run and hide? He swung the bag over his shoulder and headed out of his bedroom.

In the kitchen, Dad was still in his boxers, open dressing gown flapping about him as he dashed from sink to fridge to bread bin, doing a hundred things at once. Malcolm Hope was a one-man parenting machine. The sight wasn't pretty.

'Would it have killed you to wash the pots?' asked Mr Hope, as a growing mass of bubbles frothed in the filling sink. 'You live here too, Richard. This isn't a hotel.'

Trick winced at the sound of his full name. Only his father and other adults used it. He far preferred Trick. Richard sounded like the name of a kid from some posh suburb, a world away from Trick's existence. His thumb tapped the remote, flicking away from the morning news. Mr Hope was over the bread board now, hastily preparing a sandwich.

'You need some discipline in your life, Richard. You need rules.'

'Yeah,' replied Trick, his voice expressionless.

'And would you put the news back on, please? I was watching that!'

Trick turned at last. 'All you ever do is moan. And look at yourself, standing there in your pants. Close your robe, Dad!'

Mr Hope wrapped the sandwich in foil and turned. 'I work every hour God sends to keep a roof over our heads.'

'I never asked you to,' mumbled Trick, and his father caught it.

'You don't get to ask, Richard. When your grand-parents arrived here from Antigua, they grafted – hard. They worked like dogs. They went without so I didn't have to. It's what parents do. That's my *job*. I pull a night shift and steal a few hours' sleep. You think you can tell me how I should be, how I should conduct myself? In my own house?'

'This isn't a house. It's a flat!'

His father held the foil-wrapped sandwich out, gesturing for Trick to take it. 'Your lunch.'

'What's in it? Ham for a change?'

Mr Hope tossed it across and Trick snatched it from the air. He shoved it in his bag.

'Straight home after school; no hanging about on street corners. And stay away from any troublemakers. They're bad news, you hear me?'

Trick opened the door and shifted the bag on his shoulder. He didn't plan to go to school today. But that didn't mean he was interested in hanging around on street corners. If his relationship with his dad hadn't been such a mess, his old man would have known that. But he didn't. Trick couldn't remember a time when things *hadn't* been this way. How could a father get his own son so wrong? Trick briefly shot his dad a look, but he was back at the sink, up to his elbows in suds.

'You don't know me at all,' Trick whispered.

Slamming the front door behind him, he danced down the stairwell, not stopping to look back.

# CHAPTER TWO

'Why you antagonize your father, I'll never know,' said Grandpa from atop his stepladder, gingerly pushing a book on to a high shelf. The bookshop was one of Trick's favourite places. It was like kryptonite to morons – the bullies from school never came here.

'You're tripping,' said Trick, his foot on the bottom rung of the ladder, holding it steady for the old man. 'It's *him* who's the wind-up merchant.'

'Tripping, am I?' chuckled Grandpa, as he retreated down the rickety steps. He patted his grandson on the head in a jokey, patronizing fashion as he stepped by. If Trick's dad had done that, Trick would have kicked off for sure. But this was Grandpa: funny, a bit of a dude, and full of interesting stories. He even used Trick's nickname. Grandpa was cool.

'I got this for you,' said Grandpa, lifting a book out

from beneath his counter. It was a hardback, featuring the image of a blue-skinned giant battling two heroes. Trick turned his nose up.

'Role-playing games? They're for kids, aren't they?' asked Trick as he popped a Tic Tac into his mouth.

Grandpa laughed. 'They're for anyone, you ignoramus.' He tapped his brow. 'It's all about using your imagination, Trick. The brain's a powerful thing; it can unlock new worlds and let you experience the impossible. You're a smart boy. This should be perfect for you. That's the player's book you've got there. I have the dungeon master's guide. We'll give it a go the next time you stay over.'

'Just wasn't sure it was for me,' said Trick as he slid the book into his schoolbag. 'I know you dig them, but I've never been mad on books.'

'Why ever not?'

'They're boring.'

Grandpa staggered as if he'd been shot by an elephant gun. 'I hear you describe books that way again, and you're out of the will.' The old man winked and smiled. 'That book's perfect for you. Fantasy, battles, myths and monsters. It's all in there. It's in *all* these books!'

Grandpa waved his hands around the stacked walls of his second-hand bookshop, his blue eyes twinkling. It was hard to believe that the old chap had left school aged twelve. He was the most educated person Trick knew. In addition to English, he also spoke French and German, and was mastering Mandarin. Everything learned from books.

'I've told you before, books are magic. They can save souls, raise spirits and provide companionship. They can set prisoners free. Books can save your life, my boy.'

'Did Mum like to read?'

Grandpa stopped what he was doing, thrown by the sudden question. When he looked back to his grandson, his blue eyes seemed a little dewy. Trick's fingers had found the pendant round his throat, hanging from the bootlace beneath his shirt.

'You still wear it?' asked Grandpa.

'Always.'

The strange black stone was the shape of a crescent moon, the outer edge smooth and polished, the inner sharp and jagged. Grandpa reckoned it was a volcanic rock, but Trick wasn't convinced by the old man's self-taught geology.

'Where did she get it from?'

Trick's grandfather shrugged. 'Who knows? But she clearly wanted you to have it. To remember her by, I suppose . . .'

The boy sensed Grandpa's sadness. 'So Mum read a lot?'

'She always had her head in a book as a child,' he smiled. 'That's why we nicknamed her Edna. *'Ead-in-a-book.'* He laughed. 'Morning, noon and night, we'd find her reading. Especially at night. She got some tellings-off for reading by torchlight beneath her sheets, I can assure you!'

Trick snapped his fingers gleefully. 'I do that with my comics!'

Grandpa's laughter slowly faded. 'I thought she was going to come and help me in the shop when she left school, work alongside me and Grandma. Nobody was more surprised than us when she joined the army. When she came home after that, she was changed.'

'Changed?'

'Smiles grew scarce. Things she'd seen overseas, I guess. Fighting.' He shrugged. 'Meeting your dad was the best thing that could've happened to her. He's a good soul, and he helped her through some dark times. And then they had you!'

Grandpa pulled Trick close for a quick hug. He was already nearly as tall as the old man, having inherited his gangly frame from his mother, but he allowed the white-haired bookseller to kiss his head.

'You were a blessing, Trick.'

'Then why did she leave us?'

'Your mum wasn't a happy person, Trick. Things just got too much for her. Your poor father worries it was his doing, that he drove her away.'

'Did he?'

'No! He looked after your mum. And you, for that matter.'

Trick considered his grandfather's words. Hanging around the old man was a way for him to get closer to his mum. Grandpa shared tales about her that only a father could have known. Trick and his dad rarely spoke about her. Cassie Hope's disappearance had cast a shadow over her family which seemed impossible to shift.

'Haven't you got somewhere to be?' said Grandpa finally.

'Nope.'

The old man pointed at the clock behind the counter. 'Ten thirty-five. I don't know much about schools but I'm pretty sure that means you're late.'

Trick laughed. 'Yeah, I was thinking of maybe heading in at lunchtime.'

Grandpa wasn't laughing. 'You keep skipping school, you'll wind up in trouble.'

'You sound like Dad now.'

'So what if I do? Your father speaks sense. What do you think's going to happen if you keep bunking off?'

'Dunno. Maybe they'll give up on me. And that's cool. Means I can spend more time here.'

Trick grinned, but Grandpa shook his head.

'That won't happen, Trick. Someone will file a report on you. That's how it begins. They'll come to your flat, snoop around. Next thing you know, you'll end up in a home somewhere, far away from those who love you. Change the record, Trick. Turn over a new leaf, starting today. Get yourself *back* into school. Work hard and be *kind* to your dad. He's an amazing, loving man, and you just don't see it. He's the real hero.'

Trick stared at the clock. Maybe the old chap was talking sense. Trick knew he could be difficult – when people *thought* that's what you were, it was easy to act like that – but maybe he didn't have to be that way . . .

Trick hopped down off the stool and threw his grandfather a wave.

'Laters, Grandpa,' he said as the old man saluted him.

'I love you, Trick.'

The bell chimed as Trick opened the door. The day outside looked a little bit brighter all of a sudden.

'Love you too.'

# CHAPTER THREE

Trick stood in the comic shop, admiring the mint-in-box action figure in his hands. A character from one of his favourite comics in all her plastic glory, dreadlocks flowing, katana strapped across her back. Trick had a ragtag collection of action figures at home, members of various superhero franchises standing awkwardly alongside one another, with the occasional King Kong thrown in for good measure.

If he had a job – say, working for Grandpa – he knew *exactly* where he'd blow his wages. He'd been known to shoplift on occasion when cash was hard to come by, but he had never taken anything from this particular shop. It meant too much to him and, besides, that new leaf had been turned over not an hour earlier. Reluctantly, he popped the katana-wielding zombie-killer back on the counter.

'You not buying that?' asked Kinnon, the bald-headed, bespectacled owner of Super Freaks.

'Not today. Haven't got the dough.'

'Want me to put it to one side? She's a rare one, and she *will* sell.'

'You'd do that?'

'As it's you.'

Kinnon took the toy off the counter and placed it on a shelf beneath the old-style till. Trick raised his knuckles, and he and the comics guru did an elaborate fist bump known to customers as the Vulcan Hand Grenade.

'This is me saying goodbye, by the way,' Trick said, passing Kinnon a handful of coins that covered his comics bill for that week.

'You taking your business elsewhere?' asked Kinnon, depositing the cash in the till. 'You're killing me, man!'

'Dry your eyes. You just won't see me in the day any more. I'm done playing hooky. Going to get myself back in school and stay there. See what all the fuss is about.'

'What next? Comets striking the Earth and the dead up and walking?'

Trick laughed. 'Figured I owe it to my old man. You'll still see me at weekends.'

'Music to my ears,' said Kinnon as Trick made his way to the door. 'Take care, Trick. And enjoy school!'

'Miracles may happen!' Trick replied as he waved goodbye.

Before he'd taken three steps, Trick was pulling out his stash to rifle through them. All were regular orders for him, his standing order of comic goodness. Sharp-shooting, web-slinging, shape-shifting and walker-hacking – all quarters were covered. With his head down and immersed in the comics, Trick didn't see his foes until it was too late.

'If it ain't Hopeless!'

Trick looked up. There were two of them, and it was the smaller one who had spoken: Danny Yeo, aka Youngblood. A career truant, Danny was the diminutive chief bully from school, and although a foot shorter than Trick he was a comfortable two years his senior. At Youngblood's shoulder stood his chief henchman, a spotty streak known as Dogbreath. He sported a badly cultivated moustache that rippled across the length of his snarling lip.

Trick felt someone bump into him from behind. It was Honey, Youngblood's girlfriend, as tough and mean as any bully he'd ever encountered. She wore a long black parka coat and her big mop of golden hair obscured her eyes from view.

Youngblood. Dogbreath. Honey. Triple trouble. Trick hadn't been expecting to see them in town, their usual haunt being the estate where Trick had grown up.

The trio had always made his life a misery. What rotten luck to bump into them! He glanced around for an escape route, but they had him trapped. To his right, beyond a railing, the traffic rolled by.

'What you been buying, Hopeless?' said Youngblood.

'Nothing,' replied Trick, trying to shove his comics back into his bag, but it was already too late. Dogbreath reached forward and snatched them from his grasp. Obediently he handed them over to Youngblood.

'Sick,' said the shorter youth. 'Been donkey's since I read *Spider-Man*. I didn't even know they still did this comic. Cheers, brah!'

Laughing, Youngblood rolled the comics up and shoved them inside his jacket.

Trick bit his lip. Fighting back would do no good at all. He'd only ever done it once in his life, and the jury was still out on whether he'd won then. That had been in middle school when the bully who'd tormented him throughout infants had pushed him once too often. He'd been known as Big Ben Barker. He'd had the beginnings of a moustache and he'd been still in short pants. For three years that brute had nicked his lunch, until Trick had finally reached breaking point. He'd gone berserk and lost it completely, beating the bully in a frenzied, uncoordinated assault. Hair-pulling, kicking, biting – it had been ugly – and it had taken the intervention of teachers to bring it to an end.

Trick broke a thumb and lost a tooth that day, but

he was never bullied by Big Ben Barker again. All that said, there were three of them here now, and going loco wouldn't solve anything. There was only one way out of this, and it would be dangerous. Youngblood's laughter subsided.

'What else you got, Hopeless?'

Trick shook his head. 'I've got nothing.'

A lie. And as his hand drifted instinctively towards the wallet in his jeans pocket Honey seized it, causing Trick to wince.

'What you hidin' from us?' said Youngblood, reaching for the younger boy's pocket as he struggled.

It was now or never.

Trick stamped down hard, flattening Honey's foot beneath his heel. Somewhere inside her trainers he heard toes crunch. She cried out, letting go of his wrist as Trick brought his knee forward. It caught Youngblood in the sweet spot between the legs, and the bully tumbled back into Dogbreath's arms with a yell of agony as Trick hurdled the railings and leapt out into the road.

Youngblood's curses followed him across the street, as Dogbreath jumped the barrier and pursued Trick out into the traffic. The rabbit looked back at the chasing pack as he reached the pavement on the other side of the road. Dogbreath was six metres behind, with his boss following. Of Honey there was no sign, her crushed toes having apparently taken her out of the game.

*One down, two to go . . .*

Trick turned into an alleyway, dashing past fire doors and bin bags as the walls closed in on either side of him. He saw the dead end fast approaching but felt no alarm. He was more than used to thinking on his feet. These were *his* streets. This was *his* world. As he neared the end of the alley, he aimed straight for a large green waste bin that was parked against the wall.

His trainers pounded the uneven tarmac as he launched himself up on to its broad lid with a bang. Without breaking his stride, Trick leapt high, his fingertips catching the edge of a flat roof, toes scraping at the bricks as he scampered up the wall. Dogbreath bounced into the big green bin behind him, scrambling on to the top while Youngblood tried in vain to follow, his shortness scotching his chances.

*And then there was one . . .*

Trick ran along a flat roof, dashing up a fire escape to a second floor. As he reached the top, he saw that Dogbreath was still on his tail. He was a big guy but he was nimble. Trick ran along the roof, passing a skylight that looked down into a shop below, the occupants oblivious to the game of cat and mouse being played out above their heads.

Ahead, Trick saw a gap between the buildings, a chasm yawning before him. He didn't slow, trusting his parkour skills to help him escape the danger. They didn't fail him. He sailed three metres forward through the air, another street whipping by beneath him. He landed on a lower roof, tucking into a roll that scattered a gathering of pigeons into flight. Then he was running once more. He looked back.

The bully followed Trick's lead, not slowing but opening his stride to leap the space between the buildings. He landed with a *crunch* and a curse, but quickly regained his feet.

*Big, nimble and not afraid of heights. Terrific.*

'Stop running, you little grunt!' shouted Dogbreath. 'You ain't gettin' away!'

Another street loomed into view ahead, but this time there was no gap to leap, no alley to hurdle. It was a main road. Trick swallowed hard. He was two floors up and there was nowhere to run. But if he was caught now it would be game over. There was no choice. His trainers tore over the stony roof as he increased his speed towards the edge.

'You nutter!' screamed Dogbreath, as Trick's foot hit the stone parapet and launched him out into the busy street.

As he hit the red metal roof of the double-decker bus, Trick thought for a moment it might propel him back into the air like a trampoline. Instead it buckled with the impact as Trick threw his arms out, momentum carrying his body forward. As his fingers gripped desperately, steel squealing beneath him, Trick caught sight of the tall bully, left behind on the building. Just as

Trick slid over the edge of the bus roof, a black cab pulled up beside it.

*That'll do the trick . . .*

Trick let go.

He bounced off the roof of the taxi and slid down the windscreen and over the bonnet. Followed by a torrent of profanities from the cabbie, Trick cut through another dingy side street that took him past noodle bars, pubs and swanky shops until he emerged, dishevelled, out into sunlight again. His heart hammering in his chest, slowly finding its regular rhythm again, Trick took a moment to get his bearings.

Across the street stood the British Museum. Huge banners exalted the museum's new show: *Warriors of the World*. Trick's attention was focused elsewhere, though. If he headed east along Great Russell Street, he'd soon be back on track. He might even make it to school before the bell went for the end of the lunch hour. An afternoon in class was the first baby step towards Trick's reformation, and that journey would begin today. He started along the pavement.

'Oi!'

Trick turned, along with everyone else in the street. It was Honey, hopping along the pavement, barging pedestrians aside as she made straight for Trick. She had her mobile phone in hand, and was no doubt relaying his whereabouts to her boyfriend.

Trick didn't hang about. He cut across the road,

horns blaring as he dodged cars and vans, and dashed between a pair of great black iron gates. In seconds he was sprinting up a broad flight of stone steps, flanked by towering columns and crowds of gawping tourists. A heartbeat later he was swallowed by the cold shadows and labyrinthine halls of the British Museum.

# CHAPTER FOUR

The main exhibition halls of the British Museum were packed with a smorgasbord of colourful characters. Two school parties jostled past each other, exchanging insults and flirtations as the teachers ushered them by. Visitors from every continent brushed and bumped into one another, coachloads of Japanese and American tourists monopolizing the exhibits. It was all perfect for Trick. Here was a ready-made jungle for him to get lost in – and, better still, to put the hunters off his scent.

Trick reached the end of a long corridor of artefacts, stopping beside a huge set of closed double doors. Two brass stanchions stood to attention on either side of the entrance, a thick red rope hanging between them, barring access. In case that wasn't enough of a deterrent, a framed sign hung from one of the heavy wooden doors, informing the public that the new exhibition would not be open until the weekend. Trick balanced on tiptoes to look back through the crowd, searching the sea of bobbing heads for signs of his pursuers.

Nothing. He was about to duck back down, a very contented meerkat, when he spied Honey's unmistakable golden moptop. Her eyes might have been hidden by her thick, bushy fringe but, judging by the way her head suddenly snapped in Trick's direction, he'd been spotted. He dropped low again, cursing his timing. He had to move fast; she'd be on him soon enough, with Youngblood no doubt close behind.

Slipping beneath the red rope, Trick tried the door handle. It turned and the door opened a crack to reveal a darkened space beyond. Trick darted through, gently pulling it to behind him. Then he turned round, eyes struggling to cut through the darkness – and almost cried out in shock.

An army of soldiers surrounded him, weapons raised to strike him down. Trick flinched, backing away and bumping into the double doors with a bang. But the soldiers didn't attack. Instead they remained frozen, their blades unmoving. Trick blinked, letting his vision become accustomed to the gloom.

Mannequins. Hundreds of them, disappearing into the recesses of the room, swallowed by the darkness. He moved forward, treading carefully along a rich red carpet, eyes fixed upon the figures, each dressed in outlandish garb. There were display cases too, loaded with artefacts from times long gone – scrolls, gems, scabbards and spearheads – genuine antiquities, presumably, as opposed to the fancy-dress outfits the mannequins were wearing.

In the centre of one glass cabinet was a dish of smooth, dark polished rock. Roughly the size of a dinner plate, it seemed somehow familiar, but Trick couldn't quite work out why. He moved on uneasily.

He'd taken maybe a dozen steps when he heard a sharp noise from behind him. The door! It creaked open and a long, straight beam of light scythed through the shadows, silhouetting two figures – one bushy-headed, the other short and stocky.

'Come out, come out, wherever you are,' said Youngblood.

'We're not gonna hurt you, Hopeless,' added Honey. 'Much.'

With that, the girl pushed the door shut behind her. It closed with an echoing *click* that sent icy shivers cascading down Trick's spine. The chill spread, gripping his heart and creeping over his chest like a flesh-eating frost. He looked around as he retreated among the army of dummies, searching for a way out. If there was one, it was hidden from view by the ranks of outlandishly dressed soldiers. Trick recognized some of them as he passed: Japanese samurai, Teutonic knights, Roman centurions and Spanish conquistadors. They were a multitude, each representing a warrior class from a different time and culture. He might have stopped to marvel at them, admiring their fierce beauty, had he not been the focus of Youngblood and Honey's awful attentions.

Trick could hear them whispering to one another, plotting their means of catching him. He winced, cold fear burning in the centre of his chest. He came to a halt against a wall, partially concealed by a scimitar-wielding Umayyad warrior. His hand went into his schoolbag, searching for something that might help him against them. Among the spilled Tic Tacs, his fingers found a biro. What was the saying? *The pen is mightier than the sword?* If only.

But then a thought crept into Trick's head. If he could distract the two thugs, there was a chance he'd escape the room in one piece. He pulled the ink cartridge out of the biro as he heard one of his foes approach.

It was Honey; the tall girl's mop of golden hair was the first thing to shimmer into view. She was pacing between the warrior mannequins, head flicking from side to side, drawing ever closer. He could hear her breathing, deep and ragged; she sounded exhausted from the chase and was possibly still limping from his stamp on her foot.

Trick had always been told never to hurt girls, a rule he'd managed to follow – until today. However, when a girl was three years your senior, had a mean streak as wide as a motorway and intended to do you serious bodily harm, the rules got a little hazy. Honey was a stone-cold bully just like Youngblood and Dogbreath, and had to be feared and respected as such.

She was six metres away. Trick clung to the shadows behind the ancient Muslim warrior, willing himself invisible as he brought the empty biro to his lips. He blew hard.

Somewhere behind Honey, a tiny mint projectile pinged off a suit of plate-mail armour, making her spin round. Instantly, she was pacing towards it, leaving Trick with a clear path back to the big double doors. He gave silent thanks to the old pea-shooter he'd got as a *Beano* giveaway when he was in junior school. He'd misspent many hours blowing dried peas at the neighbour's bull terrier. Tic Tacs were pretty much the same size and shape.

Trick scampered through the shadows, staying low to the ground. He was nearing the door and the promise of escape when the cold tightness in his chest suddenly intensified, shifting into a very physical pain. He stumbled to a halt as the icy burning sensation drew his gaze to his chest and his eyes widened with shock.

From beneath the fabric of his school shirt, a cold blue light emanated, as bright and beautiful as anything Trick had ever seen. He threw a hand over it, trying to shield the freakish azure glow from view, but it was hopeless. It shone from beneath his spread palm like a star, myriad rays arcing about the room. He looked up just in time to see Youngblood leap out of the shadows, a stanchion stolen from the entrance in hand. The brass pole swung down, forcing Trick to dive clear, striking the mannequin of a Celtic warrior, which came crashing down off its plinth on top of him.

'You little worm,' snarled Youngblood, a mad, murderous look in his eyes as the blue light cast a sickly glow over him.

Trick was torn between evading the half-pint psychopath and looking down at the glow on his chest. His hand went from his schoolbag to his mouth, positioning the biro quickly back between his lips.

'What you got there?' spat Youngblood, jabbing the pole towards him. 'Give.'

Trick gave, but not what the knucklehead wanted. Another Tic Tac rocketed from the end of the plastic pen, catching Youngblood in the right eye. The bully screamed as he reeled back in agony. Trick scrambled away, gasping for breath, only to collide with the base of one of the giant display cases, sending it toppling to the floor in an explosion of glass. He cried out as he was showered in jagged shards, feeling them lacerate the flesh of his cheek.

He curled into a foetal position, covered in ancient relics – coins, goblets, jewellery and totems. Then Trick's eyes slowly reopened.

There it was, half a metre away amid the wreckage, instantly commanding his attention. The black dish sat atop a bed of broken glass, shaking with a life of its own. The hairs on the back of Trick's neck stood on end, as if the air around him were charged with electricity. His teeth hummed and his bones ached, while the pendant on his chest vibrated against his skin.

Then he realized why the dish had seemed familiar. It was made of the same strange material as his pendant. Suddenly, one by one, glowing symbols burst into life round the plate's circumference, leaving the centre of the plate bare of markings, a black hole within a blinding halo of bright blue energy.

Trick's stomach turned in on itself and the oxygen disappeared from his lungs. The pain was unbearable, making him roll across the broken glass, flipping and flopping like a fish out of water. Through the brilliant light, Trick could just make out the twin shapes of Youngblood and Honey as they stalked towards him. The shining stone pendant suddenly rose from Trick's chest, levitating eerily before his face. The two bullies watched in slack-jawed wonder, their attack momentarily paused. Then Youngblood raised the brass stanchion once more, ready to strike his helpless prey, and Trick felt the cord round his throat go taut as the pendant whipped across him, snapping against the centre of the dish like a magnet.

The last thing Trick saw was the descending metal pole before a heavenly light exploded, blooming, blossoming and swallowing everything.

# CHAPTER FIVE

The light was blinding and absolute, cold and cleansing. *Is this heaven?* Trick wondered. The deafening silence slowly changed into a dull, distant roar, building in the boy's head and making his entire being shake. His body felt buffeted, buoyed, as if he were being carried upon a wave of brilliant energy. He might have found this comforting if it hadn't been for the peculiar tapping at his skull, a steady *rat-a-tat-tat* that didn't cease. A warmth spread through him, across his flesh and through his bones, as the deathly chill subsided.

There was something else too – a surging, soaking sensation, running over his skin and face. The liquid ran into his mouth and down his throat, causing him to hack, cough and splutter. The rapping upon his head intensified now, a stabbing staccato beat played out urgently against the back of his skull. Trick thrashed where he lay, sand shifting beneath him as he struggled to lift his aching head from the strange, salty water. As his face emerged, the sound of the sea suddenly intensified, the dazzling light fracturing into myriad colours as the sun shimmered into life against a bright blue sky.

Trick lifted a weary hand from the water to brush away the jabbing sensation from the back of his head. A flap of wings made him flinch as taloned feet suddenly disengaged from his shoulder, causing him to flop into the waves once more. Where was he? What on earth was going on? His exhaustion was absolute. He could have fallen back into the water and let the waves drag him out into the sea, if it weren't for that bird. It was a big black crow, now hopping on the shore in front of him. It jumped from one foot to the other, kicking up the golden sand before leaping forward to jab him between the eyes with its beak. Trick winced, lashing out and sending the bird dancing clear with a flurry of feathers. It cocked its head suddenly, pointing its dagger-like beak back down the beach. Trick turned his aching neck, following its gaze.

In the heat haze it was hard to distinguish where the beach ended and the sky began, but there was no mistaking the fact that a figure was running through the surf towards him. The man was about a hundred metres away; he was a few inches taller than Trick, but twice as wide, and kicked up sand and spray as he came.

He wore pitch-dark leather boots and elbow-length gauntlets as well as a pitted black tabard running down to his knees that bore the stained image of a skull. The battered helmet he wore obscured his face from view, looking like an upturned tin bucket with rivets bolted round its base. A T-shaped slit ran across his eyes and down to the chin. Most alarming of all was the mace he carried in his right hand, its chain and ball circling round his head like a deadly, spiked propeller.

Trick looked over his shoulder, back the other way, but saw nobody else on the beach. He returned his attention to the approaching man in the ridiculous outfit. Fifty metres and closing. *Surely he can't be running to me*, reasoned the boy. Whatever this man's beef was, it was hardly going to be with him, was it?

'Can I help you?' called Trick.

The man didn't answer. Nor did he slow.

Twenty metres.

The crow made a harsh, croaking squawk that sounded surprisingly close to the word 'duck'. Trick could hear the weapon now, whistling as it whirled round the warrior's head, links clinking as the taut chain spun. The man charged on like a berserk rhino, straight for the teenager.

Ten metres.

'Are you *deaf*?' said the crow. 'Duck!'

Ten kinds of shock kicked in at once and Trick finally heeded the black bird's advice. He threw himself forward as the helmet-headed nutjob lashed out with his mace, launching the spiked ball into the spot that the boy's head had just occupied. The steel star whizzed by unimpeded, making the assailant spin as if he were an Olympic hammer thrower. The man's body turned as his momentum carried him straight into the boy sprawled in the foaming water. Trick winced as heavy boots trampled over his midriff, feet tripping as the man in black went flying.

He landed on his back with an almighty splash in the surf beside Trick, grunting once as the air was expelled from his lungs and his weapon flew into the air. He grunted a second – and final – time when the mace descended, fast and hard, and the spiked ball landed squarely on the T-slit of the helmet with a resounding, sickening crunch. The metal crumpled as the weapon's head found its way through the opening to the face within. Trick shrieked in shock, scrambling clear of the fallen fighter as he backed up the beach.

Finally out of the sloshing water, the boy gingerly rose to his feet. His hands went up and down his body, checking for wounds. It had all happened so fast; his head was spinning. Moments ago he'd been in the British Museum, and now he was on a beach in the blazing sun, having been attacked by a mace-wielding maniac.

He examined the body from a safe distance. It was turning on the tide, slowly circling as the waves threatened to drag it out to sea. Trick looked towards the horizon, spying only azure water as far as the eye could see. His gaze returned to his motionless foe, the mace still firmly fixed within the helmet, the water running red around his ruined head. Trick waded out a few steps, giving the man a tentative poke as he checked for life.

'Reckon he's chum, pal.'

Trick turned, finding the big black crow on the beach, a beady eye fixed upon him. Of course: the talking bird. Trick didn't know whether to scream or cry, opting instead for a nervous laugh.

'You reckon?'

The crow bobbed its head. 'Oh yeah. He's brown bread. You gonna check his corpse or what?'

'His corpse?'

'Yeah,' said the bird, raising its wings as it shrugged. 'May as well. Ain't much use to him now, is it? And, I gotta say, you're looking a bit light on kit for a warrior. You'd be wise to loot him for what he's got. I can see he's got a nice knife on his weapon belt.'

'Yeah?' said Trick, struggling to hide the disbelief in his voice. 'Perhaps I can pull the mace out of his face too while I'm at it?'

'Strictly speaking that's a flail, mate. Your mace doesn't have a chain that links the haft to –'

'Shut up!' shouted Trick, making a dash for the bird and aiming a boot at its feathery body. The crow took flight – not far, but just out of reach of the crazed teenager. 'I can't believe I'm talking to a flipping blackbird!'

'Now then, young mate, no need to be rude,' said the feathered fellow. 'I ain't some common blackbird. I'm a crow. And the name's Kaw.'

'Course it is,' said Trick, wiping a delirious tear from his eye as the dead knight's body slowly began to disengage from the sandbank. Was he dead? Was he in hell? This was all too much for him.

'Nice necklace you've got there, mate,' said the bird, eyeing the crescent pendant round Trick's throat. Trick tucked it back beneath his shirt, out of sight. 'Last chance on old Fishbreath over there,' continued Kaw, returning to Trick's side on the shore as the dead man began to drift out to sea. 'You wanna grab his gear, now's your last chance. There's some wicked sharp stuff there . . .'

Trick didn't answer, instead watching the corpse as it rolled in the waves. He could hear his father's voice, cautionary words about the dangers of knives. *Wherever this was, did those rules still apply?* Killer knights and cockney crows: he was pretty sure he was no longer in Holborn. Trick winced as he felt something stinging his left cheek. He brought his fingers up and found a sliver of glass speared into his skin. He delicately pulled it out, turning it in his hand.

Everything flooded back to him, an info-bomb that confirmed all his worst fears: the museum, the broken cabinet, the rune-riddled plate and the pendant round his neck. He dropped the glass fragment into the water and grabbed his pendant. It no longer glowed, having returned to its smooth, black lifeless state. He turned to the crow.

'Kaw, right?'

The bird bobbed, bowing. 'At your service, young warrior.'

'I'm no warrior.'

'Sure you are. You've turned up here, just like so many of 'em.'

'So many?'

'You ain't the first. They've been arriving for ages now, battle-hardened champions from some distant land, appearing out of nowhere. You're the latest in a long line. Mind, I have to say your choice of attire leaves a lot to be desired . . .'

'This is my school uniform,' said Trick, matter-of-factly.

'School whatnow? Nope. Dunno what that is. But, if that passes for armour where you come from, you won't last a minute next time you're up against one of Boneshaker's minions.'

'Who's Boneshaker?'

'Leader of the Skull Army, the one and only Big Bad of the Wildlands. That's where you are, see. This world is his, pretty much, bar a few brave folk who fight back against his tyranny. I could do with introducing you to some of them, I reckon.'

'I don't need introducing to anybody. I just need to get home.'

'Yeah, you ain't the first newcomer to say that either. None of them have gone home, mind, wherever home is. It's a one-way ticket, see. I ain't never heard of any of you warriors making the return journey.'

Trick fought the rising panic. This was a nightmare. Perhaps he'd wake up at any moment, but he wasn't counting on it. Everything felt far too real: the salt in his mouth, the sun on his face and the sting of his cheek. He might have been suffering from an aneurysm, or be in a coma somewhere, but for the time being he was going to play this for real. If this ludicrous talking bird could help him get home – or wake up – then so be it. If they wanted a game, then player one was stepping up.

'You mentioned a Skull Army? I'm gonna go out on a limb here and say that those guys are bad news. Am I right?'

'Oh yeah,' said Kaw, ducking his head to direct his beak at the corpse on the tide. 'That's who Sharkbait was with.'

'Sharkbait?'

Trick looked back out to sea, just in time to see the body tugged beneath the surface, the thrash of a big fin dragging it down into the depths.

'Boneshaker casts a long shadow over the Wildlands. There are few places his darkness hasn't reached. Many cities and free people have been enslaved, falling under his thrall. Those who fight back have been killed, crushed or gone into hiding. Our only hope is your kind.'

'My kind?'

Kaw squawked. 'The warriors who are summoned.'

'I'm no warrior,' repeated Trick.

'Yeah, you've said that before and I ain't convinced.'

'I'm a schoolboy from London! I'd much rather run away from a fight than charge towards one.'

If a bird could smile, Trick suspected Kaw would have at that moment. 'There you go, young warrior. Not all heroes run blindly into battle. Caution can be as great a weapon as the finest blade. There are many ways to win a war.'

Trick's eyes narrowed. 'For a blackbird, you say some quite profound things.'

'Crow,' corrected Kaw. 'And I'll accept your apology once you've met some friends.'

'Friends?' Trick couldn't remember the last time he'd had one. The person who most closely fitted the bill was Grandpa and he was an *awful* long way away. 'I don't have any friends.'

'You might have shortly,' said the bird, taking flight. 'There's a place, y'see, for folk like you. Follow me!'

# CHAPTER SIX

The village of Warriors Landing was a short, stumbling walk from where Trick had been washed ashore. Smooth beaches gave way to grass-tufted dunes, hillocks that rose and fell, the ground shifting treacherously beneath his feet. More than once the boy lost his footing, slipping and sliding in a shower of golden sand. Warm rays shone down, drying the clothes on his back and leaving him with a sorry sense of disorientation. It had been October back home in London, wherever that was. Now here he was on some sun-drenched stretch of coast, having witnessed a crazy killing and engaged in conversation with a crow. Weird didn't come close.

'So what's with this village then?' asked Trick. 'How did it get a name like that?'

'It's been here for years,' replied Kaw, gliding overhead on the warm air currents. 'This has been the first port of call for many strange souls who've arrived in the Wildlands – from *your* world. The people were wary at first, as some of these folk were . . . fighty, if you know what I mean?'

'Fighty?'

'They like to scrap. With anyone, I might add. They're warriors, after all.'

'So what made the villagers trust them?'

'Some proved themselves to be honourable. A number of them did good deeds. Word spread, and soon the village became a safe haven for these brave, battle-hardened souls. They could make fine allies for a warrior like yourself.'

Trick was getting a handle on this strange world now. Medieval, armour-clad warriors were somehow teleported here to do battle, judging by the lunatic on the beach. If he hadn't known better, he would've assumed it was some fancy virtual-reality computer game. However, the stinging flesh of his cheek reminded him that things were all too real.

'How much further?'

The crow didn't answer, his eyes wide and fixed on the horizon suddenly. Trick looked up, seeing a pillar of dirty smoke rising over the next wind-blown dune. As boy and bird crested the hillock, the wrecked settlement of Warriors Landing appeared before them. Trick staggered to a halt, struggling to comprehend what he saw.

'What's happening?'

Kaw landed on his shoulder, dipping his dark feathered head. 'Boneshaker. That's what's happening, by the looks of things.'

Warriors Landing was a ruin. The village was made up of around fifty buildings of varying sizes: homes, farms and businesses. Each had been reduced to rubble, the rooftops burning and walls broken down. The largest building appeared to be an inn at the heart of the village, its thatched roof still belching dark clouds of smoke into the clear sky.

Outside this structure, a troop of thirty or so black-armoured soldiers had gathered in the dusty street, hooting and hollering. Many were on horseback, while others rolled beer barrels off the porch of the tavern, loading them on to wagons that were already heaving with white-smocked prisoners.

Trick looked away from the captured townsfolk, his attention drawn to the lush trees that flanked the road through Warriors Landing. Dark forms swung in the shadows beneath each tree's canopy. As Trick crept slowly nearer, mindful of the black-clad soldiers, he got a better look at those shapes – people, hanging by the neck. Every one of those bushy trees had been transformed into a makeshift gallows.

'Boneshaker did . . . this?'

'Not in person,' said Kaw. 'His Evilness wouldn't stoop to bring himself down out of Shadowshard to do this dirty work. No, that's the Skull Army you see before you.'

'But why?'

'Weren't you listening to me, young warrior? This village was a safe haven for your type, providing refuge for those who'd make a stand against Boneshaker. Looks like His Stinking Rottenness has had enough. His lads are here to dish out a bit of retribution.'

Trick returned his gaze to the soldiers who were seemingly preparing to leave. While many were already mounting horses and wagons, a group remained gathered before the inn. Trick's inquisitiveness got the better of him. He advanced down the road, creeping and dashing from one smoking building to the next as he drew nearer to the ruined inn. As the boy and the bird passed the trees, Trick could better see the hideous, hanging bodies. Three looked similar to one another, with dark hair, swarthy skin and wearing simple white smocks. Villagers like those in the wagons, perhaps? Trick quickly realized that the rest were dressed very differently, and his theory about the warriors' medieval origin was blown out of the water.

The first wore a torn tabard over a chain shirt which bore the image of a rampant lion. The next man looked African and was mostly naked, his flesh marked with white warpaint that swirled across his well-honed muscles. The third was a woman, her pale skin and blonde hair marking her as Northern European. Her bronze breastplate was battered, scored with a multitude of savage marks. They were all so disparate, no two corpses the same. Trick counted a dozen trees, each one occupied by the dead. They represented warriors from each and every continent, spanning time as well as cultures.

'Oi!' said Kaw, pecking Trick's ear and stirring him from his reverie. He had been so transfixed by the trees and their grim baubles that he was paying no heed to where he was heading. He was almost on the steps of the smouldering inn when he finally snapped back to attention, ducking into the smoking ruins out of sight of the soldiers.

'Sorry, pal,' said the executioner, 'but we're right out of trees. This'll have to do.'

Dead ahead, not ten paces away, another black-armoured soldier stood on the inn's porch, looping a rope over a creaking beam. A red-haired young warrior was connected to the other end by a noose round his neck, as the soldiers mounted their horses before him. Then the hangman stepped off the porch and handed the rope to his master, who sat on a snorting black warhorse behind him. Trick's breath caught in his throat.

If he had been standing, the commander would have reached well over six feet tall, although the antlers that sprang from his helmet added a further two feet to his stature. The bucket helmet obscured his face from sight, the black metal matching the plate armour that covered every inch of his body. This was studded throughout by shards of what appeared to be broken black glass, making him look as if he were covered in hideous shrapnel. The mounted giant turned in his saddle to address the huddled prisoners in the wagons. His voice turned Trick's stomach; gravel and broken glass dragged over slate.

'Your treachery has brought us here,' said the warlord as he slowly began to reel in the rope, drawing it through his gauntleted hands. 'You harbour the enemies of my master, you face his wrath. Many of your kin have been slain this day.' He paused, allowing prisoners and soldiers to glance around at the corpses in the trees and those that littered the dusty street. 'They may be considered the fortunate ones. Your fate is . . . undecided. Those of you who have been spared, know this; if you are lucky, you will endure a life of servitude upon your arrival in Sea Forge, or perhaps a swift death in Boarhammer's arena. Displease my men and you'll be lucky if you draw another breath.'

A sudden flash of lightning and crack of thunder made everyone flinch where they stood. A globe of brilliant blue light shimmered into being in the middle of the road, and a figure took shape within it. With a second blinding burst of energy, the glowing sphere was gone, and a warrior landed upon the bloodstained ground with a thump. Was this the summoning the crow had spoken of?

The newcomer's black robes were tied round his waist by a red sash, and upon his head he wore a matching turban. Trick recognized the man as a Saracen warrior, having seen the swordsmen in his favourite comics and movies. A shining silver scimitar was stowed within the stranger's scarlet belt, and the Saracen's fingers were moving towards the pommel. The warrior's pointed black beard emerged from his jutting chin, and tiny gold rings looped through the wiry hair. His eyes were wild and panicked as the mob of soldiers turned upon him. With frightening speed, he snatched at the scimitar's handle.

The commander was faster. His gauntleted hand came up from his weapon belt, a dagger in it. With a spin of the wrist it was whistling across the road, striking the newly arrived Saracen in the breast with deadly accuracy. The man dropped, dead in the dust. The warlord's grating speech continued.

'Do we have an understanding?'

The tearful, frightened mob of villagers nodded, weeping and holding one another in horror as the wagons slowly began to trundle on their way. Trick saw one child among them; she could only have been five years old, with a huge mop of jet-black hair. The kid's big brown eyes were fixed upon where Trick hid in the shadows. He wondered for a moment if the child might alert the soldiers to his presence, but instead she simply stared at Trick. What unnerved him most was that, while all the others around her wept, the girl's eyes remained dry and unblinking. It was as if she were all cried out after the horrors she'd witnessed.

The warlord continued to wind in the rope, trotting over towards the inn's porch as the hemp went taut. The red-haired youth was suddenly winched off the decking and into the air. The hanged youth's legs danced an awful jig as the black-armoured leader tied the rope round a hitching post.

'Saddle up,' shouted the gravel-voiced monster as he gave his horse a spur-heeled kick to the flank. 'We ride for Sea Forge!'

Then the Skull Army were on the move, leaving Warriors Landing burning, a dying man hanging and a schoolboy from London shaking and shivering with shock.

# CHAPTER SEVEN

The Skull Army had hardly left the village before Trick was scampering out of the smoke-fogged alleyway and up the steps of the inn. He made straight for the lifeless hanging warrior. In his haste, he tripped over an abandoned helmet that sat on the porch, but somehow kept his footing. Kaw squawked as Trick ran, taking flight and flapping furiously as the boy seized the limp youth by the legs and lifted him.

'It's no good,' said the bird, as Trick hefted the limp warrior on to his shoulders. 'He's snuffed it!'

'Peck the noose loose,' grunted Trick as he stood unsteadily with the red-haired youth slumped on his back as smoke continued to belch out of the burning inn.

'But he's gone!'

'Do it!'

The crow landed on the young man's head, twisting

his beak to pick and worry at the knot. Gradually it came apart, and the warrior fell forward as the rope came free. Trick tumbled down with him, trying to catch him before he hit the boards. The two landed in a jumble of limbs, and Trick crawled out from underneath and rolled the fair-skinned youth on to his back. He couldn't have been much older than Trick. Perhaps late teens?

Preoccupied as he was, Trick was unaware that a bare-headed soldier had emerged from an alley beside the inn. The man had clearly been relieving himself and was adjusting his plate suit as he made for the steps. His armour clanked as he stopped suddenly, alerting Kaw to his presence. The crow squawked as Trick rose and spun. Soldier and schoolboy remained motionless, frozen momentarily. Trick's eyes flitted to the helmet at his feet that had almost broken his neck; it had not been discarded after all. The soldier's grizzled face twisted into an expression of menace as he weighed up the boy before him. Then the man was moving, whipping a dagger out of his weapon belt as he bolted up the steps towards Trick. The kid was quicker.

The black helmet rocketed through the air, toe-poked by Trick directly at the soldier's face. It struck him hard and sweet in the forehead, splitting the skin as he lurched up the steps, intent on murder. Trick looked left and right; there was nowhere to go but backwards into the inn. Smoke might have been billowing out of the open doorway, but the boy had no choice. Throwing a sleeved forearm over his mouth, he ran in. The brute followed, bouncing off the door frame as he gave chase, cursing.

Fires still burned, above and around the inn's stone walls, which were all that had kept it standing. Trick dashed through the debris, running he knew not where, all too conscious of the killer on his heels. Lead the soldier in and get back out before the whole inn came down – that was Trick's plan. His parkour skills kicked in. He jumped on to a chair, his next step finding a table that instantly tilted and sent him forward. Trick leapt, hurdling upturned furniture as he arrived on the long bar at the inn's centre. The soldier followed with a great deal less finesse, throwing stools and tables aside as he pursued the boy. The crackling roar of the fire raged overhead, where the upper floors were still aflame, and black smoke rolled between the floorboards and boiled across the ceiling.

A knife hit the bar at Trick's feet, the blade quivering in the wood. He looked back at the soldier who was already pulling a second knife from his belt, a broken-toothed grin breaking up his ugly face. Trick dropped behind the bar, in no doubt that he was in mortal danger. He scanned for anything he might defend himself with. A keg the size of a bucket was stashed beneath the counter. He snatched it up, hearing the contents swill about inside.

'I got a rope with your name on, scum,' said the soldier, his voice directly above Trick. A gnarled hand reached down over the counter, seizing the boy by his hair. He cried out, launching the keg up at the man. It cracked him square in the face, the wooden container exploding as its contents showered his head and shoulders. He released his grip on Trick, wailing as his split scalp was peppered with brandy-soaked splinters. Trick didn't hang around, jumping up and rolling back over the bar as the blinded soldier smacked his bloodied lips.

'Come here, you little –'

He never got the obscenity out. A blackened beam buckled above him, sprinkling the soldier with burning embers. The moment the glowing shards glanced his saturated shoulders, the brandy ignited with a *woof* that would have put a Rottweiler to shame. His shout became a high-pitched scream as he was engulfed by flames, allowing Trick to dash for the door as the ceiling came down behind him. The soldier's cries were silenced as Trick leapt through the crumbling doorway in an explosion of dirty smoke. Kaw took flight from the porch, squawking excitedly. The whole melee had lasted half a minute.

Trick didn't stop. He dashed straight to the hanged youth's body, dragging him off the steps and into the dusty street, away from the crumbling inn. Trick bent over the body, turning his head and placing an ear to the chest, checking for signs of life. Anything.

'Told you,' sighed Kaw, as Trick retrieved the dead soldier's helmet. 'He's brown bread, ain't he?'

The bird watched the boy slide the helmet into the horse trough, returning with his makeshift bucket sloshing. Kaw hopped clear as Trick tipped the contents of the helmet over the motionless youth. The young warrior didn't react to the faceful of water. Trick sighed, dropping to his knees, the helmet rolling from his hand across the dirt. His head slumped as Kaw flapped closer.

'Fret not, kid. You can't win every battle.'

The red-haired fighter spluttered, his eyes flickering open as Trick's heart suddenly soared. The youth fixed his gaze upon the schoolboy and mouthed two words silently – *thank you* – before his blue eyes fluttered shut once more and he fell into a deep, troubled sleep.

# TOKI'S SUMMONING

## Norway, AD 787

The drum beat fast.

Toki could feel it in his head, in his heart, reverberating through his body. He looked over his shoulder, spying his brother warriors as they bent their backs to the drum's rhythm, straining on their oars as they worked together. The deck lurched with each stroke and the boat's prow cut through the waves as it ploughed along the narrow channel and shallow waters towards the shore.

As the chief's son, he was expected to be the first on to the beach, leading the raiding party. The thrill of the forthcoming battle made the red-haired youth's skin flush, and his palms sweated as he clutched sword and shield. Peering up over the prow of his longship, Toki chanced a glance.

The drum beat was quickening.

His father's chief scout had told them that the enemy's village would be deserted, that their warriors would be away on their own raiding mission. This was the way of the Viking: loot, pillage, kill your neighbour. Sure enough, there were no ships in the tiny harbour, no longboats moored at the jetty. There was no sign of life at all. The longhouses were devoid of activity. It was like a ghost town. If the warriors were away, then where were the women and children? Toki looked up at the cliffs that loomed on either side of them. The village was situated in an inlet, accessed through this rock-lined channel. He glanced back at the following longship, on which his father sailed: his expectant father, awaiting his only son's impending victory. Something wasn't right.

The drum beat grew frenetic.

Toki saw movements above, all along the clifftops, as figures suddenly emerged along their length. They carried bows with strings pulled taut, flames licking from the pitch-soaked arrowheads that were ready to be unleashed. Toki screamed to his men, warned them they were betrayed, ordered them to stop rowing; but it was too late.

He could already feel the longboat's hull scraping on the gravel of the inlet's beach. Right on cue, the arrows flew, flaming missiles descending upon each raiding ship. Toki raised his shield and an arrow struck it, almost dislocating his arm from its socket. The deck was suddenly ablaze and his comrades wailed as they were peppered with arrows. The handful of men who were crowded beside him looked to their leader.

'With me, lads!' roared the chieftain's son as he leapt up on to the dragon head carved into the boat's fearsome prow. As he jumped on to the sandy beach, he could see the horde of Viking defenders spilling from the longhouses, fully armed and prepared to fight. He spied his father's treacherous chief scout among them, thick as thieves with his foes. Toki swore to Odin that he would kill the betrayer, or die trying.

From nowhere, a blinding blue light enveloped Toki, snatching him from the air. He felt as if his lungs were charged with lightning, as if his whole being had been struck by a thunderbolt. The light grew brighter, until there was nothing, and the drums and the death were a distant, dark memory.

# CHAPTER EIGHT

While the red-haired youth slept, Trick explored the remains of Warriors Landing. The few buildings that still stood were brick-built, their roofs burnt, their inhabitants long gone. The village was a ghost town, all sign of life wiped out by the soldiers of the Skull Army. By the time he returned to the dilapidated wreck of the inn, the young warrior was sitting upright, his back to the water trough. Kaw hopped about nearby, fruitlessly scratching at the dry earth for worms. When he saw Trick approaching, the youth scrambled to his feet, teetering and threatening to topple at any moment. Trick dashed towards him, catching him by the elbow.

'Whoa, dude,' said Trick. 'What are you doing? Sit down!'

The young man shook his head, his mop of red hair flicking water in Trick's face.

'I am not Dude,' he said, punching his breast with a clenched fist, his voice hoarse after all he'd endured. 'I am Toki, son of Tulka. And I owe *you* my life, friend.'

The fist now struck Trick in the chest – hard – making him wince. Friendly it may have been, but it hurt like heck. 'Steady on,' said Trick. 'I dread to see what you do to people you hate.'

Toki's face lit up, freckles dancing across his nose and cheeks as he held his open hand out. Trick moved to shake it, only for the young man to snatch at Trick's forearm beside the elbow, gripping hard as he pulled him in close. They clashed torsos. Toki clapped Trick's back with his other hand. It seemed the manly greetings were far from over.

'OK,' said Trick, disengaging from Toki's embrace and encouraging him to sit on the water trough. 'I get it. Bear hugs, macho posturing and all that. You're worse than my Uncle Tony. You can't shake his hand without him trying to crush it.'

'Apologies, friend. I assumed you were a warrior, like me, called here to battle Boneshaker and his awful army.'

'I'm no warrior, and the name's Trick.' He raised a fist and Toki did the same, hesitantly. Trick struck it across the knuckles with his own, his greeting of choice. 'And that, Toki, is a fist bump, how we say "hello" from now on, right? No more bone breaking!'

Trick got a good look at his new acquaintance, who was ruefully rubbing his throat. The mark that encircled his neck was red and livid, and the noose had left painful lesions in his skin. Yet he was alive, having somehow survived the rope and the asphyxiation. That meant Toki was tough. He wore a rusty orange woollen tunic, tied round the waist by a leather belt, while his dirty brown leggings were scuffed and torn by a fair amount of fighting. Beyond that, it was hard to place him, although it was refreshing to hear him speak.

'Whereabouts in England are you from?' asked Trick, as the young man stood once again, this time more steadily.

'England?' Toki shook his head. 'I don't know this place. I am from Norrvegr.'

'But you speak English.'

Toki shrugged. 'I speak the language of my people, Norse, as do you. But my, you're the *strangest*-looking Viking I've ever encountered.'

'Viking?' whispered Trick in disbelief.

'It's the Wildlands!' squawked Kaw, abandoning his foraging. 'Magic runs through the rivers, the land, even the air you breathe here. This place has a funny way of mixing and making sense of your words. You speak the Wildtongue, the moment you arrive.'

Trick turned to the bird and eyed him suspiciously. 'For a blackbird –'

'Crow!' corrected Kaw.

'For a crow, you seem to know an awful lot about what's going on here.'

'A chattering rook is a mere trifle,' said Toki, elbowing Trick heartily in the ribs. 'By Odin's beard, there are such beasts in this land! The mere sight of them would curdle your giblets!'

Trick's smile slipped as he looked at the dead bodies in the trees. 'What happened here, Toki?'

The young warrior sighed wearily. 'Warriors Landing was a haven for those of us who were summoned, a place to gather and form alliances.'

'Summoned, you say? Like that guy in the turban who turned up in a flash of light?'

'Exactly like that!'

'His timing really sucked,' said Trick, glancing across to where the Saracen's corpse still lay in the street.

'Didn't it just?' replied Toki with a sigh. 'I heard tales of other Vikings, such as myself, who had passed through Warriors Landing, including the legendary warrior known as Shield Maiden. Such talk drew me to this village, and I found friendship here too. Brothers in arms, such as you and me.' He looked at the trees sadly. 'Gone now.'

Toki ran a thumb round his neck, reminded of his ordeal. 'If it hadn't been for you, Trick, I would be in Valhalla now.'

Trick felt uncomfortable. It wasn't like him to do anyone a favour, bar Grandpa, and hearing the Viking's grateful words gave him a new and uneasy feeling.

'They came last night,' Toki continued, 'while the villagers slept. We were feasting in the inn with the elders, toasting, quaffing and relaxing. We were utterly unprepared. The Skull Army swept through Warriors Landing on a wave of steel. Those who weren't killed were taken, dragged away in shackles and wagons, destined for Sea Forge.'

'What's Sea Forge? I heard the dude with the bucket of antlers on his head mention it.'

'Big city on the coast,' said Kaw. 'Governed by Boneshaker's warlord, Boarhammer. Really nasty piece of work. Back in the day he was chief berserker for His Dark Evilness, the first to the front in any fight.'

'Berserker?'

'Total nutter. Drops his defences for all-out attack, and when he goes he *really* goes. He's retired from the berserking and the battlefield these days, mind you. Sits in his palace getting fat, they say, but he still carries his spiked mace with him everywhere he goes. Surrounds himself with a motley crew from the Skull Army and has the city well within his grasp. And, as for the "dude in the antler bucket", that was Tombstone. He's Boneshaker's right hand.'

Trick shivered as he remembered Tombstone's grating, gruesome voice. 'What'll happen to the villagers he's taken prisoner?'

Kaw let out a shrill cry. 'Those who ain't sold into slavery end up in Boarhammer's arena. He always needs peasants to feed to his beasts between the gladiator bouts. Keeps the crowd happy.'

Trick shook his head, struggling to take in the barbarism he was hearing about.

'We should be wary,' said Toki, looking up and down the street. 'There were other soldiers who might have been left behind by Tombstone, including a bucket-helmed monster who wielded a flail.'

'A flail?'

'Spiked ball and chain. Wicked thing.'

'Oh,' said Trick, snapping his fingers as he recalled his encounter on the beach. 'I met that guy. Yeah . . . I don't think we need to worry about him.'

'You killed him?'

'No!' gasped Trick, horrified by the notion. 'I'm no killer. I'm not even a warrior. There's been a *massive* mistake, mate. I shouldn't be here.'

'So you say, Trick, but you showed bravery as great as any warrior when you saved my neck from the noose. You *are* a warrior, my friend – you just don't know it yet!'

Toki raised a fist and held it out. Trick reluctantly bumped it and the Viking cheered.

'So, what next?' asked Trick, directing the question to Kaw. 'Toki's free and I guess we're done here. Now can I go home?'

'I don't have those answers, pal,' said the crow. 'You want to seek out Kalaban. He's got *all* the answers, ain't he?'

'Kalaban?'

'Yeah – the Oracle. He may be able to help.'

'Let's go then,' said Trick, clapping his hands together. 'Where can we find him?'

'That ain't an easy question to answer. He turned hermit; been gone for twenty years.'

'Twenty years?' exclaimed Toki. 'How in Odin's name are we supposed to find him then?'

'Keep your helmet on, ginger nut,' squawked the bird, taking flight. 'Head up the River Tangle. He'll be waiting for you.'

'So we follow the river?' asked Trick, confused.

'It's a start, ain't it?' said the crow as he winged away. 'Look around, see what you can find! If you're worthy warriors, you'll find him all right . . .'

'Where are you going?' shouted Trick after him.

'Things to pinch, worms to catch,' cried Kaw as he vanished over the smoking rooftops.

Trick dusted himself down and slung his schoolbag back over his shoulder.

'Well, it was good to meet you, Toki. I need to get moving. If there are any more of Boneshaker's cronies about, I'd rather not be around when they turn up.' The Viking stepped alongside him. 'Umm . . . what are you doing?'

'Coming with you,' said Toki, lifting his fist expectantly, awaiting another bump. 'You saved my life, Trick. Where you go, I follow.'

# CHAPTER NINE

Warm though the day had been, the night was chilly. Trick and Toki sat before a crackling campfire on the banks of the River Tangle, the branches popping and fizzing in the flames. Their departure from Warriors Landing had been delayed as the young Scandinavian had insisted on not only cutting the dead down from the trees but also giving them a Viking burial in the still-burning ruins of the inn.

Trick had stood by and watched, bewildered. He was a schoolkid from London thrown into a world of war and horror. Nothing about the day's events sat easy with him, and as he stared into the fire he had to wonder how he'd ended up in this predicament.

A growl stirred Trick from his reverie, making him jump where he sat cross-legged. 'What was that?'

'Apologies,' said the Viking, smacking his stomach. 'My belly snarls like a caged wolf.'

'You're hungry,' said Trick, quickly unravelling Toki's old-fashioned speech before rummaging around in his schoolbag. He pulled out a bundle of foil and tossed it to his friend. The Viking stared at the crumpled, shining object with suspicion.

'Unwrap it,' said Trick with a smile.

Toki gingerly peeled the foil off, revealing the sandwiches Mr Hope had made that morning. He sniffed them, grinned and took a colossal bite from one.

'By Odin's whiskers, you bring hog roast to the feast!' he roared, spitting crumbs at Trick in the process.

'Say it, don't spray it.'

'Is there a greater pleasure than the taste of cooked hog upon one's lips?' Trick stopped himself from answering that one. The Viking passed the second sandwich over the fire to Trick.

'I gave them to you, mate. Looked like you needed them more than me.'

Toki shook his head. 'We fight together, we feast together – for tomorrow we may die, eh?' He grinned. Trick didn't. ''Tis the way of the warrior, brother. Take it, along with my gratitude.'

Trick reluctantly accepted it, tucking into the meagre meal while the Viking made short and noisy work of his portion. Indeed, Toki was making such a din as he devoured the sandwich that he was completely unaware of approaching danger. Trick wasn't quite so distracted. He saw a movement in the shadows between the trees. He heard the snap of a twig beneath a careless footfall. He caught the reflection of moonlight in the assailant's eyes. And he saw the glint of steel as the villain leapt from the darkness.

'Toki!' screamed Trick, but it was too late.

The stranger landed on top of his friend, sending the Viking crashing to the earth. For a second, time froze as Trick dropped his sandwich and took a good look at the crazed madman. His skin was blue and a mountainous mass of white hair erupted from his head and jaw. The shield and sword he wielded were tossed to one side as his grubby fingers clawed at Toki's panicked face, reaching into his mouth, tearing at his lips. The maniac's eyes rolled, wild and unblinking, his teeth gnashing and grating like a rabid dog.

'Celt!' gasped Toki breathlessly.

'Viking!' bellowed the other. Blue fingers seized Toki's head and smashed it into the ground. That stirred Trick to action.

'Hey, ya big blue nutter!' he shouted. 'Over here!'

The wildman turned Trick's way, just in time to receive a faceful of flames, as the schoolboy swept a burning brand before him. He let loose a shriek, scrambling clear of the shaken Toki as Trick drove home his advantage. It seemed to work, and the blue-skinned crazy man scrambled away from the torch.

Trick advanced, jeering and yelling at him as the attacker tripped backwards, falling into the river with a splash. Instantly he was thrashing about, head struggling to break the surface as he gasped for air; Trick recognized someone who couldn't swim straight away.

Tossing the flaming brand back into the fire, Trick made for the water's edge, only for Toki to seize him by the forearm.

'What in the name of Frigga's bosom are you doing?' cried the Viking mercilessly. 'Let him drown! He's a filthy Celt!'

Trick tore his arm free and leapt into the cold water as the river began to take the madman away. Trick had always been a confident swimmer and he quickly snatched hold of the flailing stranger. Then he was kicking against the current, one arm hooked beneath the fellow's jaw, his free hand and legs driving him back to the shore. Soon he was hauling the man through the mud, Toki unwillingly helping him as they rolled their assailant on to his back.

'They're bad news, the Celts,' muttered Toki, refusing to hide his contempt. 'Headhunters and berserkers, the lot of them!'

Pink streaks were now visible on the half-drowned man's blue skin, as his woad paint pooled around his shuddering body. He retched, coughing up lungfuls of water into the mud. He raised fumbling fingers towards Trick, who flinched. Toki stepped in, raising a fist, only for the schoolboy to stay his hand. The Celt gripped a leg of Trick's drenched jeans and squeezed, burbling a string of happy grunts in a thick Scottish accent.

'You can't trust him,' warned Toki. 'You know nothing about him.'

'I knew nothing about you either, remember?'

That shut him up. Trick turned back to the soaking stranger dripping blue paint. His white beard trembled as he tried to mouth something. Trick knelt – still wary, but giving the man the benefit of the doubt. Those big, wide eyes blinked now, transforming from wild and crazed to pitiful and pleading.

'Pig . . .'

Trick was taken aback. He looked up at Toki, whose fingers were already brushing the crumbs of bread and meat from his lips.

'You . . . you were after the *ham sandwich*?'

The Celt nodded enthusiastically. Trick stepped back to the fire, picked up his discarded butty and passed it to the dripping lunatic. He and Toki watched as the madman went to work on the remains of the boy's packed lunch.

'He attacked you . . . for a sandwich.'

Toki shrugged. 'He must really like roast hog.'

# MUNGO'S SUMMONING

## The Alps, 218 BC

Elephants were uncomfortable beasts. Stupid, too.

Mungo shifted in the hard leather saddle, wondering if anybody would mind if he simply got down and walked. He'd been locked in a battle of wills with his mount for the last five days of the march. He hated the elephant. The elephant hated him. The fact that Carthaginians used them for transport was a constant source of fascination to the blue-woad-painted Celt.

For the most part, discounting horses, animals were there to be eaten. Preferably by Mungo. Mungo was always hungry. While many warriors were motivated by a wide range of causes, from revenge, through pride, greed and vanity, Mungo was driven by something far more basic: hunger. If there was a meal at the end of a fight, he was in.

The route they traversed was a hellishly high and dangerous one. The mountainside loomed to Mungo's left, while a cliff dropped away to the right, clouds visible below. He looked behind at his travelling companions.

The other commanders all rode their own tusked and trunked war beasts as they followed him up the mountain pass. They were staring back. Their armour was swaddled in animal pelts to protect them from the harsh weather. To a man, they were mean-looking fellows hailing from warmer climes around Mare Nostrum, the Great Sea in the south. At their hips they carried shining steel swords, and they eyed the blue-skinned stranger suspiciously, not least because Mungo was barely clothed and it was snowing. A bit of snow didn't bother Mungo. He had arrived on this earth in the winter, a boy born to the blizzard, with hair the colour of snow. He was a highlander. These mountains felt like home.

His elephant's trunk snaked up once more, giving him a slap in the face. This had been going on for days, the beast constantly antagonizing the Celt. He gave it a stinging smack in return, and the monster let loose a trumpet of derision before trailing its smarting trunk in the snow.

Directly ahead of Mungo rode the Carthaginian general, a man the Celt had a lot of respect for: Hannibal. A great warrior, master tactician and legendary champion of the battlefield. Heroes such as Hannibal attracted other great warriors, Mungo being one of them. The Celt had travelled far to fight by Hannibal's side; the two shared the same enemy – Rome.

That empire had swept over Mungo's homeland and also threatened Hannibal's, and this was enough to unify them. So what if the Celt fought like a madman in battle, spoke unintelligible gibberish and ate whatever he could get his blue fingers on? The general was mighty fond of him, and that counted for much in this army. The painted berserker now travelled behind Hannibal and was a favourite of the legendary leader.

Once again, the trunk snaked, hovering before Mungo. He grinned, pleased that the beast had learned its lesson at last. The grin was short-lived. With a fierce whoosh, the elephant sprayed great globs of filthy snow at the Celt, spattering his face and making his blue woad run. Mungo could hear the other commanders laughing behind him, having witnessed the spectacle. Fuelled by anger, he reached forward, seizing the mischievous trunk in his hands and biting down hard upon the grey flesh. His teeth cut deep, drawing blood from the giant beast.

With a bellow, the elephant struck back, this time keeping nothing in reserve. The prehensile trunk caught Mungo clean across the jaw, sending him hurtling out of that accursed saddle into the air – and out over the cliff edge.

Flailing at thin air, the Celt began his fatal descent, the Carthaginians growing small and distant as he plummeted to his doom. He passed through the clouds, spinning, swearing, the waiting rocks shimmering into view. Mungo's hair suddenly stood on end as he tumbled, his skin tingling as blue sparks spluttered into life around him. There was no bone-crushing, eye-popping, meat-mashing impact with the earth for Mungo; instead, a blinding flash of brilliant blue light swallowed him, just before things got really messy.

# CHAPTER TEN

Trick stood on the gravel shore and stared across the pool, spray riding the breeze and buffeting his face. It was as if a great piece of the mountain had been gouged out and the lake had filled the space left behind. Mountain streams converged high up, before spilling over the clifftops in a torrent. A thunderous waterfall crashed down into the pool, churning it into a turbulent white froth. The source may have been on high, but this was the start of the River Tangle, without a doubt. From their vantage point on the beach, it was clear to Trick that they'd hit a wall – a towering one of granite at that. Of the hermit known as Kalaban, there was no sign.

'The crow lied,' said Toki. 'Traitorous black beast!'

'Mungo like crow,' said the Celt, smacking his lips.

They had discovered Mungo's name the previous

night when he'd finally recovered from his dip in the river. By saving the drowning wildman in the night and furthermore letting him eat his butty, Trick had somehow secured the loyalty of the crazy-haired, blue-skinned loon.

The three made a most unlikely trio. They had discovered that Mungo *really* didn't like Vikings, and that Toki's feelings were clearly mutual. Whenever Toki spoke too much – which was often, in Mungo's eyes – the Celt would resort to crude bodily gestures. These always had the desired effect of silencing the Viking. They had also discovered that Mungo was perpetually hungry, and there was little he wouldn't consider eating. All manner of bugs and slugs had been gobbled by the blue-woad warrior over the course of the day, leaving Trick feeling more than a little nauseous. The idea of crows being tasty to Mungo came as no surprise to either of his travelling companions.

'Kaw didn't lie,' said Trick. 'He led me to you, didn't he? That turned out pretty well, don't you think?'

Toki grumbled. 'He said the hermit had last been sighted at the head of the River Tangle. Well, here we are, and I see no sign of this Kalaban!'

Trick squinted. Although the cliffs were blanketed in shadow, the waterfall sparkled eerily, unnaturally, catching his eye. 'Kaw's a clever bird. He said look around, see what we can find. There's a clue here somewhere, I just know it.'

Trick turned round, searching the shore for anything that might prove helpful in their quest to find Kalaban. A large bank of reeds lined the pool's edge, some rising as high as Trick's head. He parted them, wading into the water and spying a dark shape within the waving green fronds.

If he'd hoped his companions might help, he was disappointed. The two warriors were soon locked in an argument about how best to cook a crow. It seemed there was nothing they could agree upon. The Viking and Celt were still bickering when Trick dragged a moss-coated rowboat out of the reeds and on to the gravel beach. Toki spotted the vessel and dashed over. He looked it up and down, inspecting it as if he were a car salesman assessing a dodgy motor. He gave it a boot and the stained hull rattled as Trick hefted one of two oars from within.

'She's no longboat, but she's seaworthy. What's your plan?' asked Toki.

Trick pointed the wobbling oar in the direction of the strange, sparkling waterfall. 'Reckon we should take a closer look at that. Can either of you row?'

Mungo was about to take an oar when Toki snatched it from Trick's grasp, grinning. 'I sailed and rowed on my father's dragon ship when I was but a whelp. We took that boat to the edge of the world. This puddle should prove no problem. Stand aside, Celt, and let me show you both how this is done.'

Trick was the first in the boat, moving to the prow, before Mungo unsteadily clambered aboard. The Celt seemed unhappy about their decision to take to the water, but he wasn't about to quit on them. Mungo snarled when Toki shook the boat, provoking a belly laugh from the young Viking. Bending his back, Toki pushed off, his feet churning up the pebbles as he drove the boat out into the water. He effortlessly jumped in, slotting the oars into their rowlocks on either side. Then he was rowing, propelling them forward.

'You dislike the water, Mungo? Why so? Did your mother drop you in the bath when you were a bairn? On your head, perhaps? That would explain much.'

Mungo watched the rippling surface distrustfully as they progressed towards the waterfall. Toki was about to say something else when Mungo cut him off with a rude hand gesture. It shut the Viking up. Trick grinned. At least their fighting was now just verbal sparring and offensive gesticulations, unlike the scrapping he'd witnessed last night. Still, there was time for that to change, no doubt.

'You believe the wall of water holds the answer?' called Toki, his muscles rippling as the oars cut through the water.

'I haven't a clue,' Trick replied, having to shout now to be heard over the roar of the waterfall. The three of them were soaking, mist drenching them as it rose from the churning spume. Mungo clutched the sides of the boat and the rotten wood crunched beneath his jagged-knuckled grip. The tiny vessel bounced about, the water turbulent around them. The confident look on Toki's face had slipped and the Viking eyed the choppy pool suspiciously.

'Don't worry, Mungo,' said Trick, leaning closer to the worried warrior. 'We've nothing to fear!'

'You may have spoken too soon,' said Toki, rising to his feet and drawing an oar from its rowlock.

'What is it?'

''Tis a kraken, brother,' said the Viking, readying the oar in his hands as a weapon.

Trick stifled a laugh. 'There's no such –'

The pool erupted around them as sinuous green tentacles shot up in the air. The trio were showered with water as three long, mottled limbs snaked towards them, swinging one way and then the other like cobras preparing to strike. Escape was impossible.

'Fight!' yelled Mungo excitedly, forgetting his precarious position and leaping to his feet. The mad look had returned to his eyes; the promise of battle was irresistible for the warrior. The boat rocked, threatening to tip them all overboard as the Celt lifted his shield and sword. His blade whipped out, severing the tip of one tentacle, which landed twitching on the boards at Trick's feet, oozing a sticky green sap. He recognized it as some kind of plant rather than a squid or octopus. That made it no less frightening – more so, if anything.

'One tendril each,' shouted Toki over the roar of the waterfall. 'They're fine odds. Into them, lads!'

Right on cue a further six weed-like tentacles emerged from the foaming water, joining the others as they lashed at the trio.

'You're kidding!' cried Trick, his voice breaking with panic. He fumbled clumsily for the other oar, cursing when it slipped through the rowlock and splashed into the water. He snatched at it as it bobbed out of reach, letting out a yelp as the tilting boat tipped him over the side. Trick went under, resurfacing with a splutter as an emerald tentacle coiled round his waist. It lifted him out of the water, tightening all the while, constricting him as it squeezed the air from his lungs.

He looked down at his companions in the boat. Toki's oar was broken in two as he stabbed at the whipping limbs, while Mungo's blue skin was covered in green gore. One mighty tentacle the thickness of a tree trunk struck the boat dead centre. It crumpled beneath the blow, sending the two warriors spinning into the air. They too were seized by tendrils and hoisted skyward. The weeds slithered over their torsos, binding them, tightening until their bones groaned at breaking point. Trick felt his head swim and sensed the approach of darkness and inevitable death.

'Enough!'

The voice came from the waterfall, its sparkling curtains parting as darkness was revealed behind. A tiny, bent-backed old man stood there on a stony beach, staff in one hand, the other raised palm outwards. Instantly, the tentacles ceased their attack, slackening but maintaining their grip on the three intruders. Then they were carried across the water and brought closer to the enchanted waterfall, the strange little man beckoning them all the while.

As they passed through the parted waterfall, Trick craned his neck, looking up at the roof of the cavern where jagged stalactites hung like dark daggers. No sooner had the tentacles deposited the trio upon the gravel beach than Toki and Mungo were leaping at the old man.

'Wait!' shouted Trick, but too late. Their blood was up, and for a Viking and a Celt the best defence was always attack. They went as one for the bent stranger, Mungo with his battered sword, Toki with one half of a broken oar in each hand. As it happened, Trick need not have been worried for the old man's safety.

The blue-skinned berserker charged at him full pelt, channelling everything into his assault, a blur of white-haired fury. The old man was there one second, gone the next, deftly sidestepping the Celt and leaving him to crash headlong into the cave wall. He turned smoothly to meet Toki's twin-staved attack, as the pieces of broken oar swung down towards his head. His staff became a blur, passing between the weapons and striking the Viking neatly across the temple. The pieces flew from Toki's hands as his legs came up and he landed flat on his back, unconscious. Only Trick remained standing, and he wasn't about to take a swing at the stranger. The old man gave his staff a twirl and it was transformed into a simple walking stick once again. He looked up at Trick.

'Greetings, Trick Hope,' he said, his gap-toothed smile broad and benign. 'I am Kalaban. Welcome to my home.'

# CHAPTER ELEVEN

'Your friends are hungry.'

'They always are,' replied Trick as he watched Toki and Mungo demolish a table of freshly prepared food, ripping through it like a pair of half-starved cartoon characters.

Toki stopped momentarily, his face slick with mutton grease. 'Always feast as if it's your last meal, for tomorrow you may die!'

'Cheery thought,' said Trick, all too familiar with the Viking's sage military comments. 'Another "way of the warrior" thing – I get it.'

'You're not eating?' asked Kalaban, gesticulating towards the loaded table. In addition to the mutton there were a number of roast chickens, baked potatoes and all manner of cooked vegetables. Hunks of bread and blocks of cheese stood, ready to be devoured, alongside an enormous bowl of colourful fruit. The smell was amazing, and Trick was certainly hungry, but he wanted questions answered before he dived in. He hoped his companions might leave something for him, though the signs weren't looking good.

'You had this banquet all prepared, sitting here, ready to eat?' asked Trick. 'It's almost as if you knew we were coming.'

Kalaban winked. 'A little birdie informed me of your approach.'

Right on cue, a squawk echoed in the dark recesses of the cave: Kaw. Trick managed a smile – the crow had been true to his word. He took a long look at Kalaban. The hermit was an inch shorter than Trick, his crooked back forcing him into a stooped posture. He was entirely bald, with a scruffy, spiky white beard that hung down over the bib of his brown tunic. His face was wrinkled and weatherbeaten, giving him a truly ancient appearance. Only his eyes gave him away. They sparkled with a youthful energy that belied his years.

'And the creature in the pool?' said Trick. 'Is that your pet?'

'Guard dog would be a more appropriate description. The krakenweed is there to keep those away who would do me harm. It hasn't failed me yet.'

'So are you going to tell me what's going on? Who are you? And why the heck am I here?'

'My name is Kalaban, and this is my home.'

Trick looked around at the damp cave. 'Seems to be in need of fixing up. Why did you choose this place and not something with, y'know, a roof, windows, heating, that kind of thing?'

'Ah, you're a comedian, Trick Hope. Just what my world needs: a funny man.'

Trick stepped up to the hermit. 'I'm scared, Kalaban. I've been in this weird world for a couple of days and I've seen people killed, tentacled plants and talking crows. If I didn't know better I'd think I'd gone flippin' loco.'

Kalaban smiled. 'I'm sorry. I didn't mean to alarm you. I'll try to make this easy for you. Walk with me while I tell you a story,' he said, turning to step deeper into his cave, tapping his staff on the rock as he went.

Trick followed hot on his heels, leaving his companions to their noisy feast.

Kalaban sighed deeply as he began his tale. 'This is my world, Trick Hope. I was born here, and I'll die here. The Wildlands was once a gentle place, but that peace was shattered by someone from *your* world.'

'Boneshaker.' It was a pretty solid guess for Trick; he'd heard this brute mentioned *plenty* of times.

'That's who he eventually became. When he first arrived, he was a powerful priest from a land called Mesopotamia, transported here by mistake. He quickly grew in power, recruiting an army and exploiting the superstitions of the Wildlanders, bending them to his will. Those who weren't in thrall to this priest took a stand against him. I was one such warrior.'

Kalaban's eyes sparkled as he spoke.

'He and I fought for seven days and seven nights, our battle taking us across the Wildlands, over river and sea, mountain and meadow. On the seventh night we exchanged our final blows, shattering one another's spirits in a crescendo of steel upon steel. Blades broken and bodies weak, we each retreated, shadows of our former selves. Peace of a kind returned to the Wildlands, as the priest and I went into hiding.'

'So, what? It's all kicked off again now?' asked Trick as they walked deeper into the darkness. He stumbled, muttering a curse as he stubbed a toe. 'You not got a light back here?'

Kalaban ignored Trick's grumbling and continued with his story. 'My path led me here after the priest and I fought. His path took him to the mountain known as Shadowshard, and there he has recovered, far faster than I have.

'His dark magic has helped him, of course. The further he has delved into his evil art, the wider the corruption has spread. Not just through him, either, but through the souls of his followers. The reach of that evil is immeasurable, touching each and every corner of this once-peaceful land. The priest has rebuilt his army and slowly taken hold of the Wildlands. And the priest is also changed.' Kalaban's next words were a whisper.

'He emerged from that black chrysalis a death's-head moth by the name of Boneshaker.'

'So he's this all-powerful bad guy, right, with an army of uber-villains at his back? I get that. But what have *you* been doing, Kalaban? Have you just been sitting in this cave, twiddling your thumbs? Kaw said you'd been in hiding for twenty years. Why so long?'

Kalaban smiled. 'Hiding makes me sound like a coward.'

'Are you?'

The hermit chuckled. 'I have rested. I have recuperated. I have waited.'

'For what?'

'For *whom*.'

'For whom, then?'

'For the Chosen One, Trick.'

'Chosen One? Dude, that line's straight out of a comic book. Has the Chosen One got superpowers too?'

Kalaban glanced at Trick as he walked along. 'Maybe.'

'But how do I fit in with all this stuff and nonsense? I don't see it.'

'You're going to help us to defeat Boneshaker.'

'Defeat Boneshaker? You've flipped, mate. I just need to get back home. I'm no warrior, I'm a kid from the city who's here by mistake. I'm not here to fight.'

'Yet a fight you find yourself in.' Kalaban stopped at the back of his cave and Trick clumsily bumped into him. The old man began rummaging in a pouch on his hip, rattling the stones within. 'And as for being here by mistake – nonsense! There are no mistakes. We need to assemble the greatest team of warriors any world has ever seen to defeat the Skull Army.

'Every warrior summoned is here on merit. The Chosen One is a fine example, one whose arrival was foretold. A warrior from Boneshaker's home world is destined to defeat him, here in the Wildlands. The Chosen One will set the enslaved free, topple the Skull Army and best Boneshaker in battle.'

'You're saying this Chosen dude is from Earth? If that's true, then this prophecy could mean any of those warriors who've been summoned is the one who'll topple him.' Trick pointed back towards the banquet chamber. 'Your hero could be Toki or Mungo.'

'While there is no doubting the honour of those two warriors, they are not the hero I've been waiting for.'

'How can you be sure?' asked Trick, stumbling again and going over on his ankle. 'And, as I asked before, is there any chance of some light?'

Kalaban removed three smooth stones from the pouch and held them in his palm. Even in the gloom, Trick could see the runes upon them. The old man's smile was bright. 'The Chosen One has another name: the Black Moon Warrior.'

Toki shivered as Kalaban threw the three stones into the air. Instead of landing and clattering across the rocky floor, they began to spin round one another, as if in a vortex.

'Let us have some light for my young visitor,' said the hermit.

Blue flames burst from the pebbles as their runes came to life. Their strange fire cast a cool glow into the darkest recesses of the cave, halting Toki and Mungo in their feasting. Kalaban waved a hand before him, sending the flying stones out in an arc, better illuminating the cave wall. Trick's mouth fell open, his jaw slack with disbelief.

'What *is* this?' asked the boy.

'These cave paintings predate the written word in the Wildlands. They predict my own encounter with Boneshaker many years ago.'

The artwork covered the entire rear wall of the cave in a concentric, circling pattern. As the flaming rune stones fluttered past, sigils and images swirled out of the rock with a magical blue glow. More runes shone, humming and resonating with one another, carrying an eerie, enchanting tune. Trick's eyes followed the incredible fresco and scenes of battles burst into life as the story spiralled inwards. There was Kalaban, appearing halfway through the circling painting, a bald-headed, bearded warrior, crudely imagined by the blue light.

Trick was squinting at the glowing blue fresco, inspecting the heroic image of Kalaban. 'I see you, but where's Boneshaker?'

'The Darkness,' said Kalaban, directing Trick's attention towards an impenetrable, shifting shadow. It moved through the light in places, apparently impossible to tie down in the fresco, wild and untamed as if the very shadows were alive. Trick shivered.

'Unnerving, isn't it?'

The boy nodded, his cockiness gone.

'I've been guardian of this fresco for twenty years, learning what I can from it, studying it for any signs of weakness in our foe. The Wild Magic that runs through the Wildlands is at its strongest here; this mystical painting is integral to it. It is the cave's magic which I've channelled, summoning you and your kind to my world. This cave holds the key to the defeat of Boneshaker. It foretells the rise to power of the Lord of Darkness. Likewise, it reveals his downfall . . . by the hand of the Chosen One.'

Trick saw it, dead centre in the heart of the cave painting, pulsing with that weird azure illumination. Many warriors, kneeling round one of their own who was haloed by a great dark globe.

'The Black Moon Warrior,' whispered Kalaban. He snatched the flying stones out of the air and tapped the gobsmacked schoolboy in the chest with a bony finger. Trick looked down at the crescent stone pendant on his chest, shining with that same sickly blue light.

'That would be you, Trick Hope.'

# CHAPTER TWELVE

'This is quite an armoury, old man,' said Trick as he drew a helmet out of a chest and tried it on for size.

''Tis a dragon's hoard!' added Toki, his voice alive with wonder.

The treasure room was another circular cavern with a babbling stream running through its heart. Torches burned in sconces in the walls, casting their light over the twinkling mass of booty. Precious metals and gems littered the chamber, coins of gold, silver and bronze carpeting the stone floor. Weapons of all shapes and sizes were stacked about, scimitars and shields, bows and battleaxes.

Mungo stood beside a rack of swords, biting each one in turn. Trick hoped he was checking the metal's integrity as opposed to actually eating them. Nothing the Celt put in his mouth surprised Trick any more.

There were so many weapons underfoot, he had to be careful where he stepped. He narrowly missed tripping over a quarterstaff and landing on an upturned cutlass.

'These items and artefacts were salvaged from many warriors who have visited the Wildlands, friends and foes alike,' said Kalaban. 'Some fought by my side, while others were sent by Boneshaker to kill me. They're gone now. Their weapons of war are all that remain. Take what you will. Arm yourselves for the quest that lies ahead.'

Trick seized Kalaban by the elbow, and the old man glanced at the restraining hand with equal parts amusement and contempt.

'Look, old man, I'm not here to fight Boneshaker, no matter what your magical wall of swirly light says. I'm a thirteen-year-old schoolboy from north London. I just want to get home.'

'Defeat Boneshaker and you'll go home, Trick,' said Kalaban, gently prising the boy's fingers from his arm. The hermit's hands looked frail, but they were as strong as steel. Then he placed a hand on Trick's jaw, as tenderly as Grandpa would have done. 'I know you're frightened, son. Believe me. Not every warrior who is summoned to the Wildlands is prepared for the challenge that awaits them. But know this: you have *friends* here. Allies. There are two behind you, and another stands before you. And there are more out there too, wandering aimlessly, waiting for a leader to step forth and give them a cause, give them direction.

Focus their wrath upon the evils of Boneshaker and his wicked Skull Army. That is how you get home.'

'But *how* does that mean a way home?'

'The fall of Boneshaker will open a portal, one that leads back to your own world and your own time. Every warrior I've summoned has come from a different place and era in Earth's history. Should Boneshaker be destroyed, every warrior will get a chance to go home. The sphere of blue light that snatched you from your plane of existence will reappear briefly, giving you just one chance to take that return journey. Unless you enjoy the Wildlands so much you'd prefer to stay.'

'No chance,' scoffed Trick. 'I'm going home the first chance I get.'

'Cease your riddling words for a moment, wise man,' said Toki, his brow knitted with rare concentration. ' "Every warrior I've summoned": they were your words. It is *you* who is behind all this, bringing my brothers and me into your forsaken world, without so much as a please or a by your leave?'

Mungo listened, catching the Viking's drift and sidling up alongside him. Both of the warriors were by now up to date on the details of the prophecy, and neither seemed pleased by this fresh revelation.

'Yes, I summoned each and every one of you here, to help in our efforts to defeat the Skull Army. And warriors will continue to be summoned until Boneshaker's beaten. It's the only way.'

'I had a *life*, Kalaban,' said the young Viking. 'I had a future with my people. I was destined to become a legend. Now all that is gone?'

Trick could see Toki's knuckles turn white where he gripped the sword he'd chosen. His anger was all too evident, and more than justified. Who did Kalaban think he was, plucking people from their homelands on a whim?

'All that is not gone, Toki,' said Kalaban, ignoring the enraged Viking's fury. 'Your world held its own . . . limitations. The prize in the Wildlands is so much greater, as are the foes you will face. This world of warriors is where true legends are forged. Your battle has always been here – you just didn't know it.'

'Trick is your hero, though. You said as much yourself. This prophecy of a Black Moon Warrior is about *him*, not *us*.'

'Until the Black Moon Warrior arrived, I didn't know *who* he or she was. We have the sharp-sighted Kaw to thank for alerting me to your arrival – he saw Trick's pendant when he was washed ashore at Warriors Landing. All I could do was summon the greatest warriors your world has ever known, and pray that one of them was the Chosen One. It seems my prayers have now been answered.'

'And how many warriors have fallen who didn't fulfil your prophecy, hermit?' asked the red-haired youth, looking around at the haul of weapons and armour that filled the chamber. 'Hundreds? Thousands?'

Kalaban sighed. 'I am not proud of my actions, Toki. I'm sorry if you feel cheated, truly I am. But you were summoned for a greater good. I've told you already: the Wildlands were once peaceful. They can be so again, with your help. Every warrior has his or her part to play in the coming battle. The Black Moon Warrior will need allies for the fight ahead.'

Mungo spat on the floor at Kalaban's feet. 'Mungo's mad,' said the Celt, before turning his back on the wise man. Toki sneered, unconvinced by the old man's words.

'You had no right,' he said. 'I had a life. I had a family.'

Trick clicked his fingers, changing the subject. 'If the prophecy tells of me defeating Boneshaker, that means I can't fail, right? It's my destiny or whatever – I'm bulletproof.' His hopes began to soar, until Kalaban snuffed them out.

'The future can yet be changed, child. The writing on the wall tells of our best and only hope – the Black Moon Warrior. If he fails, all is lost.'

Trick looked at the weapons that surrounded him, suits of chain and plate hanging from the walls. He felt overwhelmed, lost and way out of his depth.

'I could run away. I could hide. There must be places I can go in the Wildlands that Boneshaker can't reach.'

'He'll come looking for you, Trick. The minute you and his minion fought on the beach at Warriors

Landing, you triggered a series of events. That fight was a tiny pebble dropped into the sea, but from the ripple it created a wave shall grow. You are linked to him in some way. And let's be under no illusion: Boneshaker will want you dead. Of course, we must ensure that doesn't come to pass.'

'How?'

'We fight back.'

'I'm not a fighter!' Trick yelled, voice cracking with desperation. Mungo and Toki stopped what they were doing and stared at the old man and the boy. 'It's like none of you are listening. I don't know how to fight. I'm just a boy.'

'Nonsense,' said Kalaban, clapping and squeezing his shoulder. 'Warrior's blood courses through your veins, Trick. You just need to tap into it, uncork it like a wine.'

'Uncorking sounds horribly close to spilling it,' said Trick, flinching.

The hermit smiled once more. 'You could be as great as any warrior. You just need training.'

'And you'll train me?'

Kalaban sighed. 'Alas, time is against us. You will train as you travel. Though your greatest challenge is to face Boneshaker, that is the last part of your journey. You will face a series of quests before you confront the Lord of Darkness. Your first step takes you to Sea Forge.'

'Why must we go there?'

'Your quest is threefold, Trick Hope. First, you must head to the Broken Shield Inn. There you will encounter friends and allies who will aid you on your journey. Beware, though, for as well as companions you'll no doubt find enemies in that particular tavern. It has something of a . . . reputation. The toughest warriors in the Wildlands lodge there when they're in town.'

'And then what?'

'Second, the Broken Shield Inn is where you shall commence your search for the fabled weapon known as Ravenblade.'

'What blade?'

'It's a sword fashioned from the same black glass as the charm round your neck.'

'Ravenblade,' said Toki. 'A fine name for a sword.'

'Powerful swords deserve powerful names. This weapon was wielded by the first warrior who entered the Wildlands from your Earth, many years ago. It is blessed with great enchantment, and in the hands of the Black Moon Warrior becomes a weapon of great might. The rune stones tell me that the answer to the sword's whereabouts is in the Broken Shield Inn, hidden beneath the Skull Army's noses. You must claim the sword, Trick. It could be the key to defeating Boneshaker.'

Trick gulped. His father's words rang in his ears, cautionary tales about the dangers of playing with knives, and worse. Ravenblade wasn't a weapon for a schoolboy from London – nothing was. Trick shook his head. This wasn't him.

'It's not for me,' he muttered. 'I promised my dad years ago that I'd never pick up a knife in anger. I'm certainly not about to swing a sword.'

'If you won't, I will,' said Toki brashly. 'The sword is my favoured weapon, the hand axe a close second. She sounds like a beauty, old man. Fear not – put Ravenblade in my hand and I'll take Boneshaker's head clean off his shoulders, with or without the Black Moon Warrior.'

He gave Trick a playful nudge in the ribs with his elbow, winking.

'And what's the third part of my quest?' asked Trick, already feeling overwhelmed by the challenges Kalaban was burdening him with.

'Defeat Boarhammer,' said the old man with a toothless smile.

'Is that all?' said Trick, his voice almost hysterical at the enormity of the task.

'A huge number of the city's people are poor and enslaved, the captured villagers of Warriors Landing being examples. If they aren't sold on, Boarhammer throws them into his arena for the amusement of his cronies. He's one of Boneshaker's warlords, a big, ugly brute. He rules Sea Forge with an iron fist and a golden mallet, crushing any who stand in his way.'

'Does he have any weaknesses?' asked Toki.

'He has a fondness for his young ward, a blond-haired child who is his sister's son. He's as rotten as his uncle – the apple has not fallen far from the tree.'

'Perhaps if we grab the boy . . .?'

'I would never advocate harming a child,' said Kalaban. 'Besides which, you'll never get close to him. He's always at his uncle's side. No, concentrate on helping the downtrodden of Sea Forge. They're the key. Help them and they'll help you. Those poor souls need freeing, and Boarhammer needs defeating.'

Mungo grunted, appreciating that idea. A potential fight was always going to meet with the Celt's approval. Trick nodded fearfully.

'So you can't help me?' said Trick. 'You won't join us?'

'I'll help you, my boy. I'll give you whatever you need here to help you on your journey, and I'll come to your aid when I can via our mutual friend, Kaw the crow, but I cannot leave my lair. I must protect the cave, the painting and the knowledge within. So long as I remain hidden, Boneshaker will think me dead. That needs to continue until we're finally ready to engage him.'

'Sounds like coward's talk to me,' said Toki.

Kalaban prickled at that but didn't take the bait. 'Only I am able to read the prophecy wall and foretell what perils lie ahead. If I were to leave this place, exposing myself to Boneshaker, not only would it bring his wrath down upon me – quite possibly destroying me – but he would also find the cave and the mural. If he sees the prophecy, he'll know exactly who his foe will be.' Kalaban stared at Trick, driving home the point.

'So you send me out there unprepared?' asked the boy.

'Sadly, there is not time now to work on your warrior skills. As I said, you must learn as you go. Surround yourself with those you trust and who will protect you, such as Toki and Mungo. Watch them, study them and take what you need. Believe in yourself, my boy.'

Kalaban scratched his chin. 'In the meantime, you will need a weapon. No self-respecting warrior should be in the Wildlands without something with which to protect himself.' He looked around the armoury, bony fingers running over axes, hammers and crossbows. 'If you won't pick up a sword, what *will* you take?'

Trick looked at the quarterstaff he'd almost tripped over earlier. He slid his foot beneath it and kicked it up, catching it in the air. It was bamboo, and felt unusually light, as the centre was hollowed out, while each end was shod with shining metal. He gave it a spin. Trick had wasted many hours in London swinging a broom handle around the living room, knocking over ornaments while pretending he was a martial artist. The staff felt good. Appropriate.

'This'll do fine.'

Kalaban clattered his own staff against Trick's.

'A fine choice – a defensive weapon but deadly in the hands of an adept warrior.'

'I'm not about the deadly, Kalaban. I'd rather parry an attack than make one, and this staff looks just the trick. I just want to get out of this place in one piece.'

'You're taking the first steps in doing that, Trick. Just be aware, though: a day may come when you *have* to take up the blade.'

Trick nodded, but he didn't believe it for one moment.

'I would invite you to stay longer,' Kalaban continued, 'but, as I say, lives depend on the actions of you and your friends. Head to Sea Forge and the Broken Shield Inn. Find the warriors who may aid you, seek out the enchanted sword known as Ravenblade and break the stranglehold Boarhammer has on the city. But beware: the warlord is only one threat of many. The city is home to rogues, ruffians and pirates. The Thieves' Guild controls the Lower City, led by a villain whose name is Gorgo. Be careful to avoid any entanglements with his men. He's a killer – ruthless – and keeps the poor in their place while he grows rich from their labour.'

'Sounds like a piece of work.'

'Oh, he is. As I say, steer clear. And the road ahead is no less perilous. I have a map of the Wildlands I can give you, in addition to whatever equipment and provisions you require. Between here and Sea Forge, Grub Gulch is also to be avoided. It's home to the lightning bugs: giant insects that discharge bolts of pure, paralysing energy into their foes.'

Mungo fell in behind the old man and the schoolboy. 'Mungo eats bugs.'

'Not these ones, mate,' said Trick, patting the Celt on the back as they left the treasure room. 'They'll probably try to eat you!' He glanced at the black pendant round his neck as the half-moon stone bounced off his chest. He imagined a sword forged from the same material and wondered how powerful it might be.

'That warrior who first came to the Wildlands,' said Trick, calling ahead to Kalaban. 'Who was it?'

'You haven't guessed?' said the old man, leading him out of the cavern. 'It was Boneshaker, Trick. Ravenblade is the sword of the Lord of Darkness. And he may yet want her back . . .'

# CHAPTER THIRTEEN

The sun was blazing overhead when the travellers departed from Tangle Falls. Kalaban waved them off. There was no sign of the krakenweed, thankfully, as the trio crossed the water and went safely on their way. As they headed west into Greendeep Valley, Trick kept his eyes on the sky, searching for signs of Kaw. Kalaban had told them to keep a lookout for his feathered friend; when they were in need of help, Kaw would come and provide assistance in the old man's absence. Trick was anxious about what form that aid might take, most of his interactions with the crow having involved the two mocking each other.

By dusk they were in the heart of the wilds, with the River Meadswill rushing by on their right. According to Kalaban, south of the river was the safer terrain for the party to traverse. These were dangerous lands, even by the Skull Army's standards, home to savage tribes of hillmen. Boneshaker's men therefore avoided Greendeep Valley, favouring the northern banks instead, where they'd set up a military camp.

The trio stopped to lunch on the rugged moorland, tucking into food they'd brought from Kalaban's cave. For a moment, Trick could imagine he was back home, on a rare camping trip with Dad and Grandpa. Inevitably, those breaks had often resulted in bouts of bickering between the three of them. Trick was stirred from his reverie by Toki and Mungo fighting over the last chicken drumstick. Things weren't so different in the Wildlands after all.

'You ate the last thigh, you blue-skinned weasel!' said Toki, holding the piece of chicken high over his head as Mungo tried to snatch it from him.

'Mungo hungry!'

Trick tried to ignore them, focusing his attention upon the hills ahead. They rolled all the way to the sunset and the distant sea on the horizon, dotted with the woodland that speckled the countryside. He took the map from his schoolbag, unfurling it to get his bearings. At the mouth of the Meadswill there was Mudflatt, a ramshackle collection of docks, the best place for them to cross to Sea Forge on the opposite bank.

Kalaban had given the trio a bag of gold – enough to pay their way across to Sea Forge from the tiny river port of Mudflatt. Mungo wore the purse on his hip, charged with being guardian of the group's booty. Trick looked back to the horizon, spying smog further north on the coast – no doubt the site of the city of thieves. If danger awaited them there, he was glad he had Toki and Mungo along for company. They might have been belligerent, but they were the strongest allies he had.

Trick rolled up the map, tucked it away and rose off the grass. He straightened the dark green hooded cloak he'd swiped from Kalaban's stash and turned back to his companions. 'If you clowns are done calling each other names, we need to hit the road. We've a few more hours before nightfall. Ooh, last drumstick?' He reached over the seated warriors' heads and plucked it from Toki's hand. 'Don't mind if I do. Cheers!'

He set off walking, as his companions ceased their current conflict. It seemed he was able to diffuse their little battles. Each owed him their life, so in their eyes he was their undisputed leader. The thought made Trick chuckle, but he kept his mirth to himself. Cresting the next hill, he kept his eyes fixed on the countryside. The Skull Army might not be a threat to them here, but the wildmen most certainly were. Kalaban had described them as a superstitious, primitive people, bound to terrible traditions and old gods. If Trick and his companions could keep their heads down and reach Sea Forge without encountering them, Trick would be a happy young man.

'Is that . . . is that a woman?'

It was Toki's question; the Viking was pointing towards a cluster of hillocks to the south-west.

'Wo-man?' said Mungo slowly, white eyebrows rising.

'The figure tied to the pole on yonder hill. Rather hard to miss for a normal human, but then again you're hardly normal.'

Trick saw her now. Sure enough there was a figure bound to a wooden stake across the valley. The hill rose up out of a scrubby forested area, giving it the appearance of a monk's shaven head. Even from this distance, the fell reminded Trick of a war-ravaged landscape, bare trees broken as if by cannon fire. The pole was fixed at its summit and the woman was tied securely to it.

'Listen, guys. If we're going to help her, we need a plan of –'

The two warriors were already running, hurtling downhill to the meadow below.

'Wait!' shouted Trick hopelessly, dashing after them. 'You can't steam in there! It could be a trap!'

It was no good. Toki and Mungo were already running up the slope across the valley, pushing each other as they went, each of them keen to reach – and save – the woman before the other. Trick was a good forty metres behind them, keeping pace but unable to stop them. They ran through the sparse woodland, passing splintered, twisted trees and churned-up tracts of earth.

His companions were oblivious to their surroundings, but Trick missed nothing. He couldn't shake the feeling that they were being watched. There were animal tracks in the mud, deep and hoofed, as though an enormous beast had passed through the woods. Some of the trees bore great gashes across their trunks, as if they'd been scored by huge blades. Here and there, bleached white bones could be seen poking out of the undergrowth, the remains of animals – or worse – obscured by the bracken.

'Wait!' Trick screamed, again in vain, as he burst from the trees on to the hilltop.

Mungo and Toki were already at the woman's back, behind the stake, slapping one another's hands as they wrestled with the rope. Mungo barged Toki, sending him sprawling on to the grass. The Viking was straight back up, shoulder-barging the Celt aside. This continued as Trick dashed the remaining distance to the woman. Her jet-black hair was arranged in a bun atop her head, a white bandana fastened firmly about her brow. Her face was a mask of white make-up, reminding Trick of the collectible Kabuki dolls they sold in Super Freaks. Wide eyes pleaded with him, and she might have spoken if it weren't for the gag over her mouth. Trick reached behind her head, loosening the knot and letting the gag fall from her lips.

'You idiots!' she hissed angrily. 'I had this completely under control!'

'Wha–?' said Trick. 'I don't see what you mean, lady.'

The schoolboy felt goosebumps race up his neck, that feeling of being watched turning into a cold wave of dread. All around the hilltop, shadows disengaged from the gloom, emerging from behind trees or swinging down from branches. The figures were covered in thick, shaggy pelts, eyes glinting from within their dark, filthy faces, teeth bared as they edged closer. In their hands they carried axes, spears and drawn bows, their arrows trained upon the heroes on the hilltop.

Mungo and Toki ceased their fight when they felt flint spearheads pressed against their flesh. Trick gasped as he heard bowstrings straining, begging to be released. One of the tribesmen stepped right up to the schoolboy, his head hidden beneath a boar's tusked skull. The wildman's flint knife went to Trick's throat. He glanced at the woman who was bound to the stake. She shook her head miserably. Trick's smile was humourless.

'Now I see.'

# CHAPTER FOURTEEN

'So . . . this is nice,' said Toki.

The woman was no longer alone on the hilltop. Three more stakes had been driven into the ground, equidistant from one another, and Trick and his friends were lashed to them. Each prisoner was facing outwards, looking into the wilds as the night drew in. It had been an eventful evening. The leader – the fellow with the animal-skull helm – now stood before them, addressing them all.

'I'm sorry about this,' he said sheepishly.

'You could always let us go,' Trick said, chancing his luck.

The chieftain smiled apologetically. 'And let the monster visit my village? Feed on my people? No, that cannot happen. Die knowing that your death is not in vain. With *four* offerings for the beast, our tribe can sleep easy for many full moons. You have our thanks.'

'Would rather have freedom,' said Trick.

'Mungo mad!' grumbled the Celt, wriggling against his ropes.

'Toki too,' added the Viking, straining against his bonds.

The wildman was already departing, followed by his clan. Within moments, only the four strangers remained upon the hill, the moon rising high above them.

'My, but you are a comely wench,' said Toki, straining to look at the woman, suddenly remembering what had got them into this mess in the first place.

'Aye,' added the Celt, beard twitching as he puckered his lips. 'Mungo like wo-man!'

'You two idiots should have listened to the boy,' she said haughtily. 'I've never seen such disastrous lack of planning. I'm amazed neither of you are dead yet!'

Mungo looked crestfallen, while Toki's mouth worked silently. Neither were expecting that response, but Trick wasn't at all surprised. His hands worked feverishly, twisting within their constraints, as he craned his neck so he could better see the woman.

'My name's Trick, lady. Pleased to meet you.' She nodded her head briefly, as Trick continued. 'You said you knew what you were doing when my friends came bumbling along. What was your plan?'

He saw the veins bulge on her neck, and her stake

wobbled slightly, loosened a touch. She ceased straining, catching her breath. 'I'm still working on it.'

'Mungo bad feeling,' said the Celt suddenly.

The ground rumbled, the hilltop quaking.

'Is this a hillock or a volcano?' asked Toki.

'I think it's dinnertime,' whispered Trick as he looked down the slope to his right.

The treetops shook as something large passed through the woodland, drawing closer to the summit. They all heard the deep snorting and snarling, and felt the earth trembling beneath each terrible footfall. Then the trees bowed to one side, parting like curtains as an enormous beast leapt out of the forest.

The monster was the size of a house, a shuddering mass of muscle and fur. Its wiry pelt bristled as four powerful legs launched it up the incline, trotters scraping away the turf. The beast threw its head back, shaking its tusked jaws from side to side as it let loose a grunting roar that rose to a delirious squeal. Slobber flew, showering the prisoners on the hilltop. Then it lowered its head, red eyes ablaze, and charged towards the nearest: Toki.

'Pig!' shouted Mungo.

'Really? Where?' the Viking screamed back sarcastically.

As the monstrous tusks came to gore him, Toki lifted his legs and lashed out. His right foot booted the beast across the snout with a mighty crack, sending it staggering to one side. Trick watched, still working on his ropes, impressed by the gutsy actions of his friend. When the monster brought its head back, the Viking booted him the other way with another scissor-kick to its dribbling whiskery nose.

'Pig get mad!' said Mungo, chuckling. That was enough to draw the giant boar's attention. Its red eyes now focused on the blue-skinned warrior.

'Cheers,' whispered Toki breathlessly, as the monster turned on the Celt.

It got close and let loose a roar, spattering Mungo in stinking spittle. He roared back, silencing it momentarily. It lashed at him with a tusk, making him contort on the post and shift his body to one side. Having missed its target, the boar's head was suddenly alongside him, its eye beside his face. Mungo launched his head towards it, butting the bright red pupil with a resounding squelch. The boar wailed again, this time in agony as it staggered between the four stakes towards another warrior . . . Trick.

With dread, the schoolboy realized the boar was behind him. He felt its breath on his neck, its teeth and tusks raking down the stake behind him. He stretched the rope that held his hands taut, feeling the boar's massive jagged teeth catch against the hemp. They cut through the bonds as sure as a knife, sending the boy collapsing to the ground.

He scrambled backwards down the slope as the

monster continued forward, squeezing between Trick's vacated stake and the one that held the woman. Her post was pushed to one side, loosened from the earth, as the gargantuan pig stalked towards Trick. The woman heaved hard, pushing her back into the stake and working it the other way, trying to worry it free. All the while the beast advanced. Its trotters struck the ground, forcing an exhausted Trick to roll one way and then the other, evading the monstrous feet. It reared up, ready to strike a crushing, killing blow, as the boy gave a scream of horror.

Then a shape passed over the moon at the beast's back: a figure still fastened to a stake. The woman leapt high, soaring, flying on a deadly trajectory. Then she was descending, sliding free of the giant spear, her jump executed to perfection. The stake sank into the boar's neck, drove down through its throat and emerged beneath its jaw. Its squealing death rattle caught in its chest as it skewered into the earth beside Trick. The woman landed gracefully in one fluid motion, extending a hand to the stunned schoolboy. Trick took it gratefully.

'Kazumi,' she said. 'Delighted to meet you, Trick.'

# KAZUMI'S SUMMONING

## Japan, AD 1184

Kazumi ran.

The Samurai Bride, that was what they called her. Before each and every battle, her preparations included the painting of her face, as befitted a bride upon her wedding day: a mask of white, with tiny ruby-red lips. This was Kazumi's quirk, her tradition, her dark sense of humour. It was her superstition. She was married to her naginata, the long-bladed spear that was her weapon of choice, and when she had become a samurai in the service of the Minamoto clan she had vowed never to take a husband.

Now she found herself a key player in the Battle of Awazu, running across a frozen field, her painted face no longer pristine. Blood spattered it – her enemies' blood, not her own – and the fight was far from over. She had sworn allegiance to General Yoshinaka, and for very many moons had enjoyed a life of privilege. That life was over now.

She and her master were on the run, from his own family no less. Emperor Go-Shirakawa had sided with Yoshinaka's cousin, Yoritomo, and the clan leader had sent his vast army after his own blood. And here Kazumi found herself, loyal to a man the Emperor wanted dead. She had no future. Only death awaited. She could yet have a say in how that played out.

Separated from her fellow samurai and hounded by a horde of Minamoto clan foot soldiers, Kazumi danced across the ice-packed earth. The corpses of those she'd slain lay about her, many missing their heads thanks to the deadly reach of the Samurai Bride's naginata.

Suddenly she was spinning, knocked off her feet and skidding along the ice. Her left shoulder screamed with agony. She bent her head and saw the arrowhead protruding above her breast. The warriors shouted behind her, pointing out her location as more arrows hit the ground around her. She got back to her feet, stumbling and staggering as she found a dead horse to hide behind.

Placing her naginata down before her, Kazumi knelt and composed herself. Reaching behind her, she snapped the arrow shaft where it was buried in her back. Then her fingers were at her chest, bloody fingernails gripping the steel tip. She gritted her teeth, pushing away the pain as she worked the arrow through her shoulder. She felt the shaft grate against her collarbone, heard it squeal and suck as it emerged from her flesh. With a pop it came free, turning the snow pink before her.

The shouting grew louder. They would be upon her in moments. Kazumi had a decision to make, and quickly. Her hand went to her hip where she kept her tantō knife. It was gone, lost in the prolonged battle. She cursed, picking up her naginata once again. So be it. She would die fighting. She would not allow them to take her alive.

Bounding over the horse's corpse, she found a dozen foot soldiers waiting for her, swords raised. She whipped out the naginata, making them all recoil as one. Kazumi saw their murderous grins as they realized they had the samurai surrounded. They raised their weapons and prepared to charge.

'Let this be swift,' Kazumi whispered to herself.

Suddenly the enemy soldiers covered their faces as a burst of light illuminated them. Some dropped their weapons and ran in fear, while others prayed to their gods. Kazumi looked up. Directly overhead a globe of brilliant azure light had appeared, unnatural sparks playing off its spherical surface. Before she could wonder any further, the ball of lightning dropped, swallowing her up entirely and overpowering her senses. The brightness took her, and the Samurai Bride was gone.

# CHAPTER FIFTEEN

'Hog roast!' bellowed Mungo, letting loose a triumphant, joy-filled holler.

The villagers cheered as the Celt began an impromptu jig round the roaring fire, while the slain boar roasted on an enormous spit at his back. The tribesmen came forward, carved great slices off the haunches of the roasted beast, and handed out generous portions to one another. Music was played, mead was quaffed and wildmen joined the blue-skinned warrior as he led the merry dance.

Trick sat nearby, Kazumi to one side of him, Toki on the other, eating heartily and accepting the gifts of the villagers. Each was thanked with a crown of flowers, while garlands were draped round their necks. Babies were brought forward to receive their blessings, while those children who could walk crept up, keen to touch the heroes who had freed their people. As nights went, this one had seen a tremendous reversal of fortune.

'We can't thank you enough,' said the chieftain, stepping up to the three seated warriors.

'Just keep filling my mug,' said Toki, holding it out so a villager could top it up, 'and we'll say all's forgiven.'

The chieftain stared at the carcass as it turned slowly, smoking on the spit. 'We have been tormented by that monster for many years. Now, not only is the beast butchered but we have enough meat to last us through winter!'

Toki polished off his mug and held it up once more, stifling a belch as it was refilled again.

'We're not after your thanks,' said Trick. 'We just need to get to Sea Forge. Perhaps you can point us in the right direction?'

'The quickest way may not be the safest,' said the chieftain, as his tribesmen danced past, daubed in Mungo's blue woad. 'Do you mean to avoid the Skull Army?'

'Yep,' said Trick.

'These hills are ours, but Boneshaker controls the land around the coast and north of the river. The foothills of Greendeep Valley are very exposed. The agents of the Lord of Darkness will see you coming from miles away. If you mean to cross the Meadswill at Mudflatt, follow the river itself for the remainder of the way. It's rockier; you'll find more cover there. You would be wise to travel at night.'

'And our provisions? Our equipment?'

'We shall return them to you – and more – when you depart.' Mungo streaked past, bare blue flesh flashing by in a blur. 'And could you ask your friend to put his clothes back on? He's scaring the little ones.' With that, the head of the tribe bowed low and returned to the festivities.

'It's Boneshaker you're after?' asked Kazumi.

'Indeed, wench,' said Toki in his deepest, most masculine voice. 'And not just Boneshaker. First on the list is Boarhammer, the Lord of Sea Forge. We mean to crush the fiends, like nuts beneath our heels.' He balled a fist and slapped it into an open palm.

The unimpressed Kazumi ignored him, directing her questions to Trick. 'I too have an axe to grind with this Boarhammer, preferably upon his skull.'

'You've got a beef with him?'

'My travelling companions and I had set up camp in Greendeep Valley. When I returned from hunting I found that Boarhammer's men had paid a visit. My friends' heads awaited me. On spikes. Yes, you could say I have a beef with the Lord of Sea Forge.'

'Revenge,' said Toki. 'I like it,' he added, sinking his mug of mead.

'It seems we have shared goals,' said Kazumi to Trick. 'Let me accompany you, join you on your quest. This would be mutually beneficial for both of us.'

'Umm ... what's your weapon of choice?' asked

Trick, attempting unsuccessfully to sound knowledge-able in front of the samurai.

'I fight with the naginata.'

'The what now?'

'It's a pole-arm with a blade at the end. Good for parrying as well as striking from a distance. I noted that you favour the quarterstaff.'

Trick scratched his head. 'Yeah. I'm kind of learning on the job. Bit of a noob, really.'

'I don't know what a noob is, but I can help you master the weapon. I trained with a bo staff in my youth, before graduating on to the naginata. I will teach you as we journey, impart my knowledge. I expect obedience, discipline and diligence.'

Trick smiled. That was four they now numbered. 'Sweet.' He raised his fist. Kazumi looked at it with suspicion.

'He wants you to punch him,' said Toki grumpily.

Kazumi nodded, taking him at his word, and threw her fist. It connected with Trick's chin. And that was that for the boy from London for one night. He slept the sleep of the just and glass-jawed.

# CHAPTER SIXTEEN

After a further day of rest, Trick's adventuring party finally took to the road. There was only one flaw in the chieftain's suggestion of travelling at night. Great though this was for evading the attentions of Boneshaker's scouts, Trick found the darkness overwhelming. This was nothing like night back home. He couldn't go anywhere in London without light pollution illuminating his way. The Wildlands had no such man-made glow in the midnight sky.

With the moon hidden by clouds, their progress was stumbling and slow, dependent upon guesswork. None of the four had any local knowledge. All they knew was that they needed to follow the rocky passages along the side of the river, and eventually they would arrive at the shanty port of Mudflatt.

'Tin-head lost,' chuckled Mungo from the back of the party, as Toki led them through the night.

'Cease your buzzing, Bluebottle, lest I swat you,' replied the Viking as he picked a path through a narrow ravine, leading the way. 'You forget, I sailed to the edge of the world, navigating by the stars in the most storm-tossed seas!'

This only made the Celt laugh louder. 'Tin-head funny. Tin-head lost!'

There was no reply from the Viking. Instead he forged on, squeezing between the walls of rock as they descended deeper through the corridor of stone. Trick could hear the sound of the river nearby, a distant roar that hinted that they might indeed be heading in the right direction.

'Are they always like this?' whispered Kazumi as she walked behind Trick.

'Sadly, yes. They swing between annoying and infuriating. It's never dull.'

Their chatter was interrupted by the cursing of Toki as he stubbed his foot against a rock.

'Whassat?' asked Mungo from the rear. 'Tin-head need Mungo's help?'

'Shut your trap, Dungbreath,' replied Toki, struggling to regain his composure. 'I'm merely suggesting we stop for a moment to take water. We've been marching for hours.'

He wasn't wrong. Trick could feel the ache in his legs and welcomed the chance to find a rock to perch on. Toki craned his neck, searching the sky for stars. Trick didn't have the heart to point out that whatever stars were up there were unlikely to correlate with those back home on Earth. Who knew what kind of constellations twinkled overhead?

Kazumi passed her waterskin to him. Trick gratefully accepted it and took a measured swig. Then she was climbing up the jagged incline to a ledge overhead. She looked up and down the ravine, scouring the darkness for signs of movement. The Japanese woman was a tough cookie, humourless and hard as teak. The two had sparred back at the wildmen's village for long, arduous hours. The muscles in Trick's arms still hummed from exertion and the pounding she'd given him with the blunt end of her naginata. Still, he felt he was getting the hang of the bamboo staff. If he could master such a weapon, perhaps they'd stop asking him to take up a blade.

He passed the skin back to Toki and leaned back against the rock, closing his eyes for a moment and thinking of home. Dad, in particular. Usually when he thought of his old man it was with annoyance. Not now. He missed him, especially his smile. Things weren't so bad at home after all. Only now did Trick realize how good life had truly been.

He hoped he'd get the chance to return to that poky

flat in north London and repair their damaged relationship. Or at the very least wake up from his nightmare. Perhaps he hadn't dashed into the British Museum after all. Maybe he'd missed the double-decker bus when he leapt from the rooftops, and this was all some wild coma-induced hallucination. That was what happened in films, right?

Trick was snapped back to the present by a tickling sensation on the back of his right hand. He looked down to where it rested, spying something crawling across it. Although it was very dark, the bug cast a green glow as it wriggled and squirmed against his skin. Trick smiled, rolling it into the palm of his other hand and lifting it to his face for closer inspection. It was the insect's abdomen that was bioluminescent, just like glow-worms back home. Only this was bigger than anything he'd seen in England. It was about three centimetres long – a real whopper.

'Whassat?' asked Mungo, peering round Toki to get a look.

'Some kind of glow bug or firefly. Cool, isn't it?'

The Celt smacked his lips. 'Mungo eats bugs.'

'Don't you dare,' said Trick, shielding the insect from the Celt. He wondered if his dad was remembering to feed Shelob, his pet tarantula, in his absence. He hoped so. Insects wigged out plenty of people, but not Trick. And they appeared to make Mungo's stomach growl.

'Mungo hungry!' bellowed the blue-woad warrior,

striking his sword against the rock face and gurning wildly. The sound echoed up and down the ravine.

'Keep it down, fool,' said Kazumi from where she perched overhead, 'or you'll alert our enemies to our presence.'

Trick was staring at the bug, fascinated. By the light of its abdomen, he could see that all the hairs on the back of his hand were standing on end, as if charged by static. That wasn't all. The fillings in his teeth seemed to ache as he brought the creature closer to his face, as if electrical fields were rolling off the insect. A blinding spark crackled suddenly from the bug's abdomen, illuminating the immediate area. The insect lurched across his hand, gobbling up a big fat fly that had been electrocuted by the surprisingly large bolt of pure energy.

'Man, that is overkill,' Trick muttered.

'Mungo blind!' wailed the Celt as Toki pushed him away, preventing him from lurching into him. 'Whassat?'

'The bug. Lightning came out . . . of . . . its . . .' Trick's words trailed away as he suddenly realized where they were. The chittering noises in the darkness were an additional clue, as the inhabitants of the ravine were drawn to Mungo's noisy shenanigans and the glow bug's butt-flash. They came out of the fissures in the rock, up from the cracks in the ground, squirming out of the deep black shadows. The noises came from behind them, back the way they'd come, a rising din of hideous burbles.

'Grub Gulch!' said Trick, remembering Kalaban's warning. 'We're in Grub Gulch! We need to move – now!'

He jumped up, grabbing Toki and throwing him forward through the ravine. The Viking didn't object, dashing on with his sword held ahead of him defensively. That was the only way to go. Retreating would bring them face-to-face with the gulch's inhabitants and they weren't top of Trick's sightseeing list.

Then Trick grabbed Mungo, and the warrior's eyes widened in alarm as he was pulled along. The Celt struck his head on an overhanging rock, and landed on the floor with a thump. Trick heard the jingling clatter of coins as the money bag on Mungo's hip burst with the impact. Trick saw a shape rise high behind Mungo, separating from the gulch wall, as he tried hopelessly to retrieve the spilled coins. Mungo looked up, stunned, as Trick held up his bug, hoping it might cast light over the situation. That did the job, and then some.

One after another, a horde of insect rumps began to hum into life, answering the call of their tiny brethren. And these were *big* bugs. The warriors seemed to be in a sea of lanterns, shimmering and growing in intensity; the hellish insects were almost a metre long. Mandibles clapped, legs tapped and gelatinous bodies bulged and rippled. And there, behind Mungo, was the mother of all monstrous bugs. Its huge body was bloated, lights flashing within an enormous egg sac that writhed with a million tiny pupae.

The Celt screamed and raised his sword, the metal gleaming.

'No!' yelled Trick, but it was too late.

Before he could strike the giant grub, a lightning bolt arced from the queen's shuddering abdomen, connecting with the steel and sending sword and warrior ricocheting off the rocks like a snooker ball. He landed some distance away, white hair and beard smoking, eyes glazed over.

The insects rolled forward, a wave of hungry, yammering pincers and maws that sought out the warriors' tasty flesh. As the mandibles snapped, Trick danced, bouncing off the walls of the ravine with sure-footed free-running skills. Fingers and feet found the rough rock, snatching purchase and saving his skin. With each jump he evaded the lightning bugs and their deadly mouths, sensing them snapping at his heels as he leapt through the air. The rocks suddenly crumbled in his grip, sending him tumbling to the gulch floor in a shower of dust. He looked up at the queen. A second bolt was charging in the monster's body, ready to be launched at Trick.

It never came.

Kazumi leapt down from on high, the wooden shaft of her naginata gripped in both hands. The weapon's metal blade carved a deep, bloody gash down the queen's armoured thorax, sending her reeling backwards, stinking goo hissing from the wound like water from a burst pipe. She gave an awful, gut-curdling cry that almost made Trick vomit. He buckled, legs weak, as the mass of bugs surged forward to defend their mistress.

'Run!' roared Kazumi, pushing Trick on his way. The two ran blind, scooping up a stunned Mungo and catching up with Toki. Then they were sprinting, scrambling, fleeing the squirming, screeching melee of hideous bugs and grubs.

# CHAPTER SEVENTEEN

Trick stood on the jetty, staring out across the water towards the smog-shrouded city. The mouth of the River Meadswill was perhaps five kilometres across, and the fast-flowing tide and deadly currents would make it a perilous swim. In the fading light he could just make out Sea Forge's towering outline, hulking over the horizon like a sleeping stone titan. Over Trick's left shoulder was his schoolbag, while in his right hand he gripped his quarterstaff. He shook his head wearily. He was truly a most unlikely-looking hero. This was a nightmare he'd given up expecting to wake from.

Along the shore, Trick could see smaller settlements, dwarfed by the chaotic sprawl of Mudflatt. These little shanties made the small port look like an oasis. The group had passed through a number of these camps on their approach to Mudflatt, and each time had been shocked by what they found. The poor of the Wildlands ended up in these rat-holes, eking a living by whatever means they could. Beggars, clam-diggers and bin-rummagers, and that was just the children. Whole families were living in abject squalor while the Skull Army spread their misery and their masters – the fat cats of Sea Forge – just got fatter.

Trick glanced back to where Kazumi was speaking to the ferry master on the dock. Passengers were disembarking, and the ferry would not return until the early hours of the following morning – enough time for the captain to have his feed, drink and rest in Mudflatt. Then Trick saw the ferry master shake his head, his hands buried in his leather apron, ignoring the samurai's attempts to barter. He turned his back, clambering back on to his ferry, business with the woman concluded. His boat was the only way across and the fare was steep.

'He's a swindler,' said Kazumi, returning to Trick's side, her face set hard.

'What's the damage?' he asked as they walked back up the bank, the noise of the crowd rising as they neared the gathering in the heart of Mudflatt.

'Five gold a head.'

Trick sucked his teeth. They'd had that, and then some, in the money purse. Sadly those coins now lay on the rocky floor of Grub Gulch. His party was penniless and stranded. The cheering and jeering grew louder as they walked between ramshackle huts and tumbledown tents, the air thick with the stench of fish guts, booze and pipe smoke. Torches guttered on tall stands, marking out the space before the largest freestanding structure in Mudflatt. It looked like a big top circus tent, entirely covered in multicoloured swathes of cloth. Trick and Kazumi pushed through the throng, returning to where they'd left their companions. Toki looked over his shoulder as the schoolboy sidled up to him and Mungo, nodding a brief greeting.

'Any luck?'

Trick shook his head. 'We need twenty gold.'

Toki and Mungo looked at one another, before returning their attention to the arena. The raucous crowd were assembled round a large pit, the base of which was slick with mud and puddles. Coins changed hands around the pit's edge as merchants and fishermen placed bets, and bookmakers gleefully accepted the crowd's coins. On the far side of the pit, before the huge garish tent, a fat man sat on a raised wooden dais, clapping his pudgy hands as the money was deposited in a strongbox at his feet.

'There's going to be a fight?' asked Trick incredulously, as the crowd worked itself into a frenzy.

'Fight!' said a wide-eyed Mungo beside him.

'Reckon it'll get messy too, judging by the look of that brute!' added Toki as he peered into the pit.

The man below was tall and rangy, his face obscured by a great dreadlocked mane of hair. He was bare-chested but wore a leather kilt that was knotted with studs of metal. He held an axe in one hand and a shield in the other, which he struck noisily together. Above him, a huddle of vicious-looking and equally lanky hillmen roared their encouragement from the pit's edge.

'Who's he fighting?' asked Trick. Toki pointed towards the fat man's tent as a figure appeared from beneath the colourful fabric. He didn't so much walk as prowl. The fat man stood, clapping a hand on the fighter's back as he stalked past. He wore what appeared to be a jaguar skull and pelt over his head and body; the cat's mouth was stretched wide and the warrior's face poked out from within. The crowd chanted his name: *Zuma! Zuma! Zuma!* He was clearly their favourite, and seemed content, focused, horribly relaxed. He didn't even appear to have a weapon. He gave Trick the chills.

'Champion,' said Mungo. The Jaguar Warrior looked across the pit, his eyes lingering on them as he seemed to pick out Trick and his friends in the crowd. Then with a somersault he was gone, landing in the muddy pit below.

'Was it me, or was he looking our way?'

Kazumi sneered. 'He's arrogant. That will be his downfall.'

'Not so sure,' said Toki. 'If he's the champion, he won't have got the title by accident.'

'We don't even have anything to wager to win more gold,' said Trick, shaking his head.

'You know, if one of *us* were to fight him, we could win passage across the Meadswill with our winnings,' said Kazumi.

'Can you beat him?' asked Trick.

'The fool doesn't even have a weapon,' said Kazumi. 'I expect even Toki could beat him.'

The Viking glowered at her put-down, but Trick was looking at the warrior in the jaguar pelt. He *was* watching Trick and his companions, ignoring the baying mob above the pit. Surely he couldn't hear what they were discussing over the tumult and hubbub? Suddenly the crowd hushed.

The fat man on the platform rose, his jewellery jingling as he kicked the lid on the chest shut.

'The gold is in: let the fight begin!'

The giant dashed forward, axe raised high as he let loose a war cry, his companions cheering him on his way. Zuma remained motionless until the last moment, when he suddenly dived, darting between the giant's legs. His hand flashed out, leaving a trail of welts on the hillman's inner thigh. The brute hit the pit wall, winding himself, before turning round.

He charged the Jaguar Warrior again, his axe scything down, only for Zuma to sidestep and rake his hand across the man's exposed belly. Again, he left red ribbons behind. Not deep, just superficial. He did this again and again, as the slower, bigger man failed to place a blow, although it could only be a matter of time before he connected.

'He can't keep dancing,' said Toki. 'That axe will hit soon, then we'll see the colour of the catman's innards!'

'New champion,' added Mungo, the two in agreement for what appeared to be the first time ever.

'I wouldn't be so sure,' said Kazumi. 'Watch as the poison takes effect.'

They all saw it now. Gradually, the giant was becoming sluggish. He seemed exhausted, unnaturally so, the axe suddenly heavy in his hands as his enemy skipped round him, still out of reach. The Jaguar Warrior's eyes flitted to Trick's once more, locking his gaze, as a smile flickered across his dark face. Then he was pacing round the pit in a fearless strut as the hillman dropped to his knees, wheezing, the axe falling from his hands along with his shield. His skin was shining with sweat and blood, tongue lolling out through his dreadlock-covered face.

Still the crowd chanted Zuma's name as they looked to the fat man on the stand. He nodded and gave the signal, thumb raised to the Jaguar Warrior. Zuma leapt forward, flashing past the giant, hands reaching out as he went. He caught the man round the neck, twisting his head with a crack. The smaller man landed deftly as the big man toppled lifelessly into the gore-spattered mud. The crowd jeered deliriously, before quietening as the fat man spoke.

'Should there be a challenger among you who wishes to face my champion, Zuma, you know where to find me!' At this there was a chorus of shouts as numerous warriors in the audience shouted out their desire to enter the pit. The trappings of champion were enough to draw any fighter to the filthy arena, it appeared.

'In the meantime, many thanks for your participation. And your gold,' he added with a chuckle, turning and stepping back into his tent. Two enormous men-at-arms picked up the strongbox and followed him in, the flaps falling shut as they disappeared.

'So who's going to fight him?' asked Kazumi, prompting more bickering from Mungo and Toki, each of them desperate to face the Jaguar Warrior.

'Shut up,' hissed Trick, his mind working overtime. He couldn't believe any of them would be in such a hurry to meet their end. 'There might be another way, without any of us getting hurt.'

The chanting continued as more gold was exchanged in the crowd and fights broke out among bickering gamblers. The hillmen clambered into the pit, recovering the body of their fallen brother, as Zuma stood in the centre, accepting the applause of the audience. His keen eyes remained fixed on the boy in the crowd and his three companions, as they plotted and schemed.

# ZUMA'S SUMMONING

## Mexico, AD 1519

The Spaniard stumbled, splashing through the swamp with panicked strides. There was a wail behind him as the last of his companions fell – his fellow conquistadors had all met the same terrible fate. Across his shoulder, the man carried an open chest that brimmed with gold. In the crook of his left arm he gripped his upturned helmet; this too was overflowing with jewellery fashioned from the precious metal. The temple had appeared to be unguarded, the hoard there for the taking. More fool the Spaniard and his companions. They hadn't reckoned upon the beast that guarded the Aztec gold.

He looked back as he ran, clambering over the exposed roots of mangrove trees and sliding over muddy banks. He had to keep moving, to put distance between himself and the temple. If he continued in this direction, following the morning light, he would reach the beach where his landing party had come ashore. Then he could return to the jungle with more men, more weapons. But for now he simply had to shake his foe off his trail. His enemy was out there somewhere, a demon in the jungle that attacked in the darkness.

Had the monster followed the conquistador? Or had the Spaniard given it the slip? He clambered along the edge of a mosquito-infested swamp before collapsing against an enormous mangrove. The soldier paused for the briefest moment to catch his breath and look back the way he had come. It was a mistake.

The arrow punched clean through his breastplate, breaking the flesh below his ribs. The Spaniard grunted, wheezed, then stumbled down the banks of the incline, hitting the thick swamp with a heavy splash. It was like quicksand, slowly taking hold of him and pulling him down.

He struggled to free himself, but his ornate steel breastplate was weighing him down. The poisoned arrow was already working its dark magic, slowing him, making his internal organs shut down. The chest of gold remained afloat next to him, as did his helmet, but they were also sinking. The Spaniard was sinking faster though.

He snorted when he saw a shape emerge from behind the roots of the giant mangrove tree. Its skin was golden, spotted with black marks, its teeth white and deadly. A giant cat of some kind, here to watch his demise. It rose, tall on its hind legs, staring down at the dying man. The

Spaniard spat mud from his mouth as the sucking pit dragged him ever deeper. He could see that this was no beast now; it was a man, wearing the skin of a jungle cat. The pelt covered his arms and the clawed paws hung over the Aztec's clenched fists. He carried a bow and a quiver on his back.

The Spaniard begged for help, straining with all his might to raise a hand from the stinking swamp. The Aztec saw this and, grabbing a root of the mangrove, lowered himself, reaching out towards the temple robber. The conquistador managed a panicked smile, his hope rising. It was extinguished in a flash when the wild man seized the chest of gold, dragging the half-sunk box back across the swamp to the safety of the shore. Through the dark open maw of the catskin hood, the Spaniard saw the man smile.

Then the light came. The Spaniard imagined this was his Lord coming for him, ready to take him to heaven. He closed his eyes before the blue light, accepting that his suffering was over and he was going to a better place. Tranquillity was only a heartbeat away. Still the pit sucked him down, the gloopy mud surging into his throat and choking him.

The conquistador's eyes flicked open. The Aztec – and the bright light – were gone. The chest of gold remained on the bank, untouched. Then the thieving Spaniard was swallowed by the mangrove swamp, his slow, agonizing death anything but peaceful.

# CHAPTER EIGHTEEN

Beneath the starlight, Trick crouched at Kazumi's feet as the samurai's naginata touched the back of the tent. It eased through the fabric as the blade descended, cutting a neat vertical incision. Trick glanced left and right, spying the silhouettes of Toki and Mungo in the shadows; they would remain on lookout in case anyone else arrived upon the scene.

The fat merchant's soldiers were stationed on the wooden dais at the tent's entrance, leaving the rear unguarded. This was where Trick could be of use. His parkour skills had helped carry him across numerous London rooftops; his agility had always been his strength, and it would be invaluable this morning.

'In and out,' whispered Trick. 'We grab the chest and go. It's only the gold we're after, remember? The ferry leaves in a short while. Nobody needs to get hurt.'

'So you say,' replied Kazumi, holding the cut wall open as Trick slipped silently through.

The interior of the tent was dimly lit, with hooded lanterns placed intermittently around the enormous open chamber. Shifting walls of sheer fabrics and velvet curtains hung from the ceiling, and fluttered in the breeze that followed the intruders in. Cushions and pillows littered the floor, and the smell of burning incense made Trick cough. Kazumi shot him a cold glare.

Through the silk fabric they could see the hulking figure of the merchant, lying on an enormous round mattress. They parted the material, stepping stealthily closer, wary of any baubles or bottles that might be underfoot. Trick kept his eyes locked on the man, alert for signs of stirring, while Kazumi followed, naginata at the ready. Her keen gaze searched the rugs around the bed, scouring the chamber for the fat man's stash. There was no sign of it.

'Looking for this?'

The two of them turned quickly towards the voice in the shadows. A shape slowly disengaged from the darkness; it was the Jaguar Warrior who had fought in the arena, and he had the strongbox under one arm. In the other he held a strange wooden sword studded with sharp jagged stones. They were glassy and black, not unlike the pendant round Trick's neck.

'Put it down slowly,' said Kazumi, twirling her naginata, 'and I promise you a swift death.'

'I'm putting nothing down,' grinned Zuma, nodding towards the motionless merchant. 'One shout from me and the rest of his men come running.'

'So why haven't you called them?' asked Trick, wondering what game he was playing.

'You want the gold, I understand that. To get across to Sea Forge. For what purpose?'

'You seem to know our intentions well enough already,' said Kazumi.

'Your friends are not subtle. I hear and see things.'

'So, what? You want a bribe?' asked Kazumi. 'You can have my blade instead.'

The Jaguar Warrior raised his wooden sword. 'You want to dance, woman?'

'Wait,' hissed Trick. 'You haven't alerted the merchant's men yet. There must be a reason. What do you want from us?'

'I would join you.'

Kazumi snorted. 'He lies.'

The Jaguar Warrior pulled his face into a mock frown. 'Did Boarhammer upset you? Or has the mean Boneshaker been calling you names? I suspect your fight lies elsewhere. Mine is not here either. I've kicked my heels in this turd-riddled pit for months, waiting for an opportunity.'

'Opportunity?' asked Trick.

'Pay me and I fight for you, by your side.'

'A mercenary?' scoffed Kazumi.

'A soldier of fortune,' corrected Zuma.

'You have the gold already,' said Trick. 'You could just take it.'

'This is a trifle. There's more in Sea Forge, I wager. A damn sight more.'

'You want a share of it?' asked Kazumi.

Zuma chuckled. 'As you appear to be on some noble quest, I'll take more than a share. I'll take the lot.'

'Why do you want all the gold?'

The Jaguar Warrior stepped closer, his eyes wide and shining with a yellow glow. 'What kind of Aztec would I be if I *didn't* want all the gold?'

Trick's mind whirred with vague recollections of tales of Aztec warriors and their love of the precious metal. It made sense.

'You get the gold if you fight for us,' said Trick, holding his fist out.

'You would *trust* him?' exclaimed the samurai.

'What choice do we have?'

'We could kill him.'

'You could try,' said the Aztec.

'Say the word,' hissed Kazumi.

'Swear you're with us,' said Trick, stepping between them, staring the Jaguar Warrior down. The man bumped fists, the first of the warriors to successfully respond to the greeting. He lifted his wooden sword.

'My macuahuitl is yours.'

With that, he strode past them towards the slit in the

tent wall. Trick looked back at the merchant on the bed, where the fat man had remained motionless throughout their encounter. Why wasn't he moving?

'Is he sleeping? Or have you . . . killed him?'

The Jaguar Warrior stopped by the slashed fabric and glanced at the schoolboy. 'If he were sleeping, would that make you feel better?'

Trick didn't answer, but his eyes were wide and fearful.

'Then he's sleeping,' said Zuma with a dark smile before stepping through the torn tent wall. 'Come, or you'll miss the boat.'

# CHAPTER NINETEEN

The ferry arrived in Sea Forge by dawn's early light, the smog shimmering with a dirty yellow glow. Buildings loomed, their silhouettes shrouded in a filthy veil of fog. The harbour was already a hubbub of activity, crowded with ships of all shapes and sizes. Galleons overshadowed fishing trawlers as the boat from Mudflatt squeezed between them, searching for a spot where it could dock. Trick looked about, amazed by the filthy splendour of the city as it towered over them.

No sooner had they disembarked than crowds of beggars were closing in. Women, children and old folk, all crying out for help, food, change, anything the warriors could spare. Trick had a stale husk of bread in his schoolbag which he handed over to an old crone. No sooner had he done so than an elderly man started wrestling with her for it, and the two quickly became lost in the crowd.

'Better to give nothing at all,' said Zuma grimly, 'than gift them something that will get them killed.'

Toki was leading them through the market traders and fishermen, sniffing out their destination. Trick looked at his travelling companions, each of the colourful warriors sticking out like sore thumbs. Not that Trick could talk – he was still wearing skinny jeans, a maroon school blazer and battered old trainers. What a group they made. Mungo was behind Toki's shoulder, insisting that the Viking was lost, while Kazumi and Zuma flanked Trick.

'Those two know where they're going?' whispered Zuma. 'They're two arrows shy of a quiver.'

'We were told to come to Sea Forge, so that's where we've come.'

The group passed by a row of gibbeting cages, each one occupied. Some of the accused still lived, though they had been beaten and starved. Signs were tied by cord to the hands and feet of many of the men. They each bore the same legend: THIEF. Fearful, weary faces watched the group as they passed by.

'Your plan was to come here, then what?' asked Zuma. 'And who gave you advice? You're very trusting.' He paused beneath a swinging gibbet, the thief within the metal cage murmuring for mercy. 'Some might say foolish.'

'Hold your tongue,' hissed Kazumi. 'Trick is our leader.'

'And who made a *boy* your leader?'

Kazumi snarled. 'You challenge him, you challenge us all.'

Zuma chuckled. 'No offence was intended. I'm just concerned by your . . . uncertainty about your direction. I'm hired to help – it'd be good to know the next step.'

Trick chewed his lip. The group was headed to the Broken Shield Inn for three reasons: to recruit more warriors, to find Ravenblade and to put a plan into action to topple the warlord Boarhammer. However, he was in no hurry to divulge everything Kalaban had told him at his Tangle Falls hideout. After all, his other companions were by his side out of loyalty and camaraderie. The same couldn't be said for the Aztec. Gold had brought him on to the team.

'Nobody's keeping you here, Zuma,' said Trick, turning to the Jaguar Warrior and giving him a confident stare. 'You want to stay, maybe you should show a little trust of your own.'

The man raised his hands peaceably, shutting up. Trick felt his chest puff out, pleased to have managed the mini uprising. Ahead, Toki and Mungo had come to a halt outside a rickety shack that seemed to be held together by gull droppings. Parchment sheets covered a noticeboard on one filthy wall, including a wanted poster that bore the image of a character known as the

Shield Maiden. Apparently, escaping the deadly prison of the arena was deemed a crime in Boarhammer's eyes. This breakout had led to a bounty on her head of two hundred gold. Toki pointed at the parchment.

'Shield Maiden! My Norse kin – she is here, in the city!'

'Two hundred gold,' said Zuma, his eyes lighting up as Toki glowered at him.

A man sat on the doorstep, smoking a long twisted pipe as he looked out over the docks. A sign swung above his head bearing the words HARBOUR MASTER.

'Can I 'elp you?' he said, blowing a choking cloud of smoke into Mungo's face.

'Old man!' said Toki in a loud, boastful voice. 'Where might one find brave soldiers of fortune who would overturn a tyrannical warlord?'

Trick rolled his eyes, pushing his way past the not-so-subtle Norseman towards the bemused official.

'Excuse me, sir. We're looking for a particular tavern. Could you help us, perhaps?'

The harbour master sucked hard on his pipe. 'Ain't from round 'ere, are ye?'

'We came to you for answers, not questions,' said Zuma, tossing a bronze coin into the old man's lap. He pocketed it swiftly while Trick glanced at the Jaguar Warrior. He shrugged. 'Not like I gave him any gold, is it?'

'I might be able to help you,' said the old harbour

master. 'There are plenty of taverns and inns in Sea
Forge where you'll find a fighter or two.'

'The Broken Shield Inn,' said Trick. 'Have you heard
of it?'

'Who hasn't? It's where the gladiators drink. A tough
old dive is the Broken Shield. You want to go straight
down Kipper Street, right up Lobster Lane and you'll
find it overlooking Speaker's Square.'

'Right you are,' said the Aztec. 'And you never saw
us, right?'

The harbour master arched a bushy white eyebrow
until Zuma tossed him a second coin. 'Never saw who?'
he said, looking lazily away.

'Good man,' said the Jaguar Warrior before turning
back to Toki and Mungo. 'Lead on, fools.'

As they walked, Trick noticed many black-armoured
soldiers passing through the crowds, intimidating the
locals. The Skull Army. They were a mean-looking
bunch, their dark shields and breastplates daubed with
garish flashes of colour: bloody eyes, yellow fangs, blue
flames and green tears. Perhaps these marked out their
rank or the platoon they belonged to. Either way, Trick
wasn't in a hurry to be questioned by one of them. His
memories of his encounters with the pair at Warriors
Landing still made him shiver.

A wall of rock rose behind the docks on which a
second city seemed to sit above the first. While the
harbour was full of ramshackle fleapits, the higher

towers and mansions were clearly homes to the wealthy and influential of Sea Forge. An enormous arena perched on the clifftop overlooking the entire harbour, flags fluttering from its curved walls. Gates at the base of the cliffs stopped the poor from rising higher, and a winding rocky road carried those with money up out of the smog. Trick shook his head wearily.

When the party finally reached Speaker's Square, they found it heaving with bodies. Trick kept a firm hold on his schoolbag, knowing full well that pickpockets were probably at work around him. If they came near him, they'd be getting a staff to their downbelows. Everywhere he looked, he saw beggars and homeless souls, blocking every doorway and loitering in every alley. This was squalor, like something from a Dickens novel. Market stalls sold goods fresh and foul, captains called for crewmen, and crazies stood on boxes, preaching to the passing masses. To his surprise, one voice seemed to find Trick's ears over the din, and he stood on tiptoe to see over the ocean of heads.

'The Black Moon rises! The Chosen One comes! Evil's end is nigh!'

Trick gasped. Was he talking about *him*? Mention of this Black Moon certainly tied in with what Kalaban had said. A brute stepped before him, blocking his line of sight. Trick ducked, stepping into a woman carrying a basket of fish heads and almost bowling her over. He apologized, back on his toes as he searched for the owner of the voice, but there was no sign. Someone seized him by the elbow, making him jump.

'Come,' said Kazumi.

'But the voice —' began Trick.

'The inn is this way and we are separated from our companions. Let us escape the crowd.'

He was led through the throng, closer to the cliffs and the inn. The Broken Shield was extraordinary: three storeys high, with parts of it constructed from timber, while others were carved out of the rock face it stood against. The occupants of this part building, part cavern spilled out on to the veranda, ale sloshed down the steps and shouts came from within. High above the door a sign swung from rusting chains: a great black wooden shield with a dark, dirty sword buried through its middle. Toki, Zuma and Mungo stood before the inn, waiting for Kazumi and Trick.

Trick looked back at the bustling crowd and blanched. He kept seeing Boarhammer's men-at-arms moving among the civilians.

'They're everywhere in Sea Forge,' replied Zuma with a derisory sniff.

'I've got a bad feeling about this,' said Kazumi, her hand reaching for the naginata on her back as she squinted across Speaker's Square. 'I spy the black helmets of the Skull Army bobbing in this sea – there are sharks among the sprats.'

'Into the inn, then,' said Zuma, backing away towards the Broken Shield.

Mungo and Toki needed no further prompting, and stepped across the booze-soaked threshold. Zuma followed, with a wary Trick and Kazumi in tow. The boy looked back as he went in, unable to shake a rising feeling of dread as he entered the Broken Shield Inn.

# CHAPTER TWENTY

The Broken Shield Inn was a dive of the lowest or highest quality, depending upon how one looked at things. Sawdust, broken bottles and teeth littered the floor, while the stench of tobacco and stale ale permeated every nook and cranny. The few lanterns that lit the interior barely penetrated the gloom, and every snug, stool and bench was occupied by brutish-looking men of all shapes and sizes. Trick stayed in the middle of his huddle of companions, aware of how conspicuous and young he looked in such an intimidating place.

Mungo sidled up to the bar, nearly knocking a grizzled-looking fellow off his stool as he ordered five ales from the innkeeper.

'So who exactly are we looking for?' asked Zuma, drawing Trick's attention away from the door they'd entered through.

'We were told that we would find warriors here, among other things,' said Trick.

'Other things, eh?' said the Jaguar Warrior. 'Could you be any vaguer? I suspect all you'll find here is fleas and fights. This is a dead end, boy.'

Zuma turned and reached past Mungo for one of the mugs of ale. It was empty, as was the one beside it. And the third and fourth. He watched in disbelief as the Celt quickly downed the fifth jar before clattering the mug on the bar top. He smacked his lips merrily.

'More beer!' he hollered to the innkeeper.

'You're an animal,' whispered Zuma.

Mungo belched in his face, making the Aztec grimace. The Celt squinted at the jaguar pelt that adorned Zuma's head for a moment, before grinning. 'Stupid cat hat.'

The man on the stool beside Mungo suddenly leaned in close, wobbling. A gladiator's helmet sat on the bar before him, surrounded by empty mugs. He looked unsteady, as if he hadn't left his stool or the bar for hours, perhaps days. 'Watch yourself, Celt, or feel my trident up your bum.'

Trick saw the weapon, resting against the stool, its three blades rusty and disused.

'Roman,' sneered Mungo.

'I'm with my deranged friend on this one,' said Toki in agreement.

'If there's one thing worse than Celts it's Romans,'

added Zuma. 'Especially those who can't handle their mead!'

The gladiator punched his own breastplate. 'Talk to me that way, would you? I am Crixus, champion of the arena!'

'Champion of drunken old sots, more like,' laughed Toki.

'I shall have my crown back, one day,' Crixus grumbled, slurping his next drink.

Trick let them bicker. He felt the hairs on his neck tingling, as if he were being watched. He surveyed the Broken Shield. It looked like an audition for pantomime villains: pirates, smugglers, assassins and lowlifes. Deals were being done, dark deeds plotted, as blood money, ransoms and stolen goods were traded. Kalaban had told him that he'd find Ravenblade here and warriors who would fight for him. Trick wasn't convinced he'd find either. Through the crowd of conmen, killers and ne'er-do-wells, Trick caught sight of a silhouette at the far end of the bar, swathed in black except for his eyes. He sat alone, and didn't even have a drink in his hand. Could he be another of the warlord's men? Through the tumult and chaos, Trick felt the stranger's burning gaze upon him. Someone walked in front of Trick, and when he'd gone so had the stranger.

'I reckon Boarhammer has agents here too, just like in the street,' Trick whispered to Kazumi. 'Reckon I just spied one back there, watching us.'

'You're sure?'

'Yep. Seems nowhere is safe.'

Kazumi's smile was humourless. 'The moment you arrived in the Wildlands you put safety behind you. Our foes are many and danger is all around, often closer than you might think.' She gave Zuma a dark look, which the Aztec missed.

'Keep your eyes and ears open,' said Trick. 'Kalaban said we'd find answers to our questions in this tavern. We'll find warriors here, and we'll find Ravenblade. Someone here must know about the sword, Kazumi. The hermit wouldn't have sent us here on a wild goose chase.'

'See what you can find out – ask around, but be careful,' said Kazumi. 'There may be enemies here, but there are also allies, hiding in plain sight. We just need to find them.'

Trick spied Mungo sinking another pint as his altercation with the gladiator rose in volume. Allowing the Celt near the bar might not have been the smartest move. Zuma and Toki were standing beside him laughing when the Roman swung his mug, missing Mungo and catching the Jaguar Warrior across the back of the head. The pot shattered, sending the Aztec to his knees, stunned.

The two weren't friends, but Mungo clearly took exception to this assault on Zuma. His wild white hair was a blur as he butted Crixus square in the face, and the gladiator's nose crumpled as he was catapulted back into Toki. The duo crashed into a mob of men behind him. More fists flew, curses were traded along with stools and within a few frantic moments the interior of the Broken Shield Inn had descended into a riot.

Trick felt someone seize his cloak, twisting the hood so tightly it transformed into a noose. He spluttered, allowing his enemy to pull him in close. As he did, Trick turned, bringing himself nose-to-nose with the fellow who had grabbed him. His hairy face was riven in two by a jagged scar running from temple to chin, straight through a pale white eye. Trick brought his knee up, connecting with the brute's groin and making him loosen his grip instantly.

The boy whipped out his quarterstaff, whirling it in a sweeping arc. It caught limbs and torsos as more of the thugs moved towards him, but quickly pulled back as wood struck bone. There was the flash of steel as a knife came out, and one wiry rogue ducked past the scything stick. Trick contorted, twisting as the blade flashed by.

The man came again, going for a reverse swing as Trick backed towards a filthy window. Before the dagger could strike him, the man cried out as Kazumi's naginata ripped his back open. Trick saw the samurai for a fleeting moment, before she disappeared under a flying table. He was about to run to her when the one-eyed, hairy thug who'd first attacked him re-emerged from the melee. He came fast.

Trick dived backwards, smashing through the window and out into the street, leaving his quarterstaff behind. He felt his schoolbag catch on the splintered frame; it was torn from his shoulder as he fell on to the ground. More of the inn's customers rolled across Speaker's Square and the inn's tarnished sign creaked on its chains overhead as the sundered shield threatened to come crashing down on him. The one-eyed man followed, squeezing through the window and catching Trick's trailing cloak once more.

'Got you, boy,' he gurgled, reeling Trick back towards the broken window. 'Reckon you'll fetch a pretty penny at the slave market . . .'

A dark shape flew past Trick, lightning fast, and in the next second he was tumbling loose. He looked back, catching sight of his one-eyed enemy screaming, spattered with blood and retreating into the Broken Shield. On the floor, still attached to Trick's cloak, was a severed hand, gripping the soiled hem.

He looked up as the man in black stood over him, only his eyes visible. He was clad from head to foot in dark cloth, swathed tightly round his flesh. Soldiers of the Skull Army were now appearing in huge numbers, picking off the battling drinkers and wailing beggars and hauling them away. Many rushed into the Broken Shield, and screams suddenly rose in pitch from within.

'Grab as many as you can, boys!' shouted a Skull Army captain, urging his men into the tavern. 'If they won't come nicely, kill 'em. Boarhammer wants some meat for the arena. Let's make the boss happy, eh?'

The stranger extended a hand to the fallen boy.

'Come with me or stay and die.'

'My bag! My staff! My friends! I won't leave them behind,' cried Trick.

'It wasn't a request,' replied the man, grabbing his wrist hard and leaping back into the shadows, taking Trick with him.

# KURO'S SUMMONING

## Japan, AD 1579

This was no ordinary job.

Lightning split the sky above Azuchi Castle, thunder rolled and the rain became a downpour of hellish proportions. The castle was the primary fortress of the warlord Nobunaga, Daimyo of the Owari Province and ruler of the Oda clan. For a Japanese castle it was revolutionary in design: a massive structure, with walls up to six metres thick in places, constructed from giant granite blocks. It had a seven-storey central donjon tower, while irregularly formed inner citadels provided defenders with ample strategic positions against intruders.

The castle's location was also novel. Unlike other castles – usually at the base of mountains surrounded by dense vegetation – Azuchi Castle was situated on the flattened top of a mountain, affording the Oda clan a wide view of any approaching enemy. Of course, it was staffed by Nobunaga's greatest warriors, his most trusted samurai and loyal foot soldiers. It was widely considered impregnable. Only a fool would mount an attack upon it.

This was no ordinary job.

Kuro flitted from shadow to shadow, dancing from beam to beam as he clung to the ceiling of the middle citadel. Then he was on the wall once more, a black-garbed killer creeping like a tarantula, while the guards far below were oblivious. He found the chink in the armour that he was looking for: a narrow gap, left in the wall for ventilation, intended to be too small for a man to crawl through. A normal-sized man at least. Kuro was on his belly, dislocating a shoulder to fit through the fissure, slithering like an adder through the narrowest of gaps towards the inner citadel.

Given added cover by the greatest storm for many a year, he left a trail of bodies in his wake, stretching back to the tiny provisions dock where the river ran past the base of the mountain. On the stairs, the walls, the watchtowers, the courtyard, the outer citadel and onward into the castle; death had been dealt every step of the way. The bodies were hidden, stowed in bushes and barrels, cupboards and crawl spaces. Nobody would discover them until Kuro was long gone and his job complete. The ninja was death: unstoppable, unforgiving, silent and emotionless.

Oda Nobunaga had made many enemies among the nearby clans, and the other feudal warlords were unified in their hatred of their neighbour. His success and stranglehold on the region had driven his enemies into collusion, and rival clans had pooled resources to hire the greatest ninja Japan had ever known. Indeed, the most powerful man in all Japan was one of his employers.

This would be Kuro's final job. After this, a new life awaited. His katana would be put on the shelf. The fee would not only set him up for life, but also smooth the path of a hundred generations of his bloodline. One last job – his biggest ever – that he'd been planning for six months. And now it was almost complete.

He emerged from the ventilation passage into the central citadel of the castle from above, sliding through the bamboo rafters that supported the ceiling. He reached for the blowpipe inside his jerkin, fingers finding the clip of darts upon his belt. The vaulted chamber was more than eighteen metres high, filling five floors of the donjon tower.

Far below, Nobunaga stood beside his war table, upon which a map was spread. Three of his most able generals stood to attention at his back, awaiting their master's call. Key military points were marked out upon the enormous scroll: all Nobunaga's strategies played out in miniature before he put them into action on the battlefield.

The warlord straightened, pleased with his evening's plotting. He turned to his generals, only to find them slumped on the floor in a jumbled heap. Nobunaga's jaw yawned open and disbelief was writ upon his face. The warlord cried out, raising the alarm as a figure coalesced from the shadows before him, peeling away from the darkness that shrouded the walls. Kuro sprang forward, brandishing his katana before him in a downward slash.

'Emperor Ōgimachi sends his regards!'

The sword never struck Nobunaga. The warlord spun backwards, narrowly evading the blade as it sent sparks off the flagged floor. His samurai guard burst into the room, rushing the ninja and parrying his blows. They forced him back, away from his target and out of the central citadel, a horrified Nobunaga following the melee from a safe distance.

Kuro's mission had failed. All he could do was retreat. Passing a window, he leapt, shattering the glass, and found himself on one of the castle's many terracotta rooftops. The samurai guard followed, roared on by their master. Kuro danced, dodging katanas and arrows, the rain lashing his face as he neared the edge of the roof. Beyond, nothing: just the night, the storm and the darkness. Kuro jumped out into the void.

'Kill him!' screamed Nobunaga, but it was too late.

The ninja vanished before their eyes in a flash of blue light, leaving Japan's most powerful warlord reconsidering his allegiances, thanking his deity and questioning the impregnability of his greatest fortress.

# CHAPTER TWENTY-ONE

Trick fought back the rising panic, breathing hard within his sackcloth hood. He had no idea where he was being taken, as the man in black had blindfolded and bound him once they'd escaped the bedlam of the Broken Shield. Their pace had been hurried, with the stranger shoving him frequently, urging Trick onward whenever he slowed. They had descended steps and the sound of dripping water echoed around the cold corridors they traversed.

Through his blindfold, Trick could tell that daylight had been replaced by torchlight, glimpsing flickering flames through the thick hessian shroud. Occasionally Trick heard voices, muttered greetings, as his captor passed acquaintances. None seemed concerned that he dragged a boy along as his captive. Trick eventually detected the ground underfoot change from slippery rock and stone to floorboard and carpet.

'Well then, Kuro! Take the bag off. Let's see what you caught!'

Trick felt the hood's cord slacken, then it was whipped off, leaving him momentarily blinded. His hands remained bound behind his back as he slowly blinked, taking in the surroundings. They were in a cavernous, man-made chamber, the ceiling supported by ornate stone columns. Some of the walls were honeycombed with openings, within which the ruined remains of coffins could be seen. A series of waterways criss-crossed the floor, an old forgotten sewer system winding its way through the abandoned tomb. A body floated slowly by face down, a dark trail clouding the water in its wake. Torches burned in sconces and the flickering light playing over the catacombs conjured a Haunted House vibe.

Trick felt as though he was in a Halloween funfair, and the ghoulish mob surrounding him only heightened that effect. They did not wear uniforms, unlike the Skull Army. Instead they were clad in light leather, with studded breastplates, tattered cloaks and dark fatigues. They were a ragtag bunch, and Trick saw them for what they were: burglars, footpads and pickpockets. Kalaban's warnings rang in his ears and Trick realized with dread that this was the Thieves' Guild, which meant that their master, Gorgo, wasn't far away.

The crowd parted as three men strode closer. Two nasty-looking ruffians flanked an ox of a man clad in shining steel. One had a bloated, swollen face, while the other was a rat-faced fellow. The bodyguards hissed, shoving the others aside and kicking them clear as their master followed.

Their leader's suit of plate armour caught Trick's eye – it was hard to miss when all the others were dressed in leather. Round his waist he wore a weapon belt loaded with a dozen deadly knives. He held one in a big paw, flicking blood from the blade; he was responsible for the corpse in the water, Trick figured. His black-clothed captor stepped away from him, blending into the shadows of the stone pillars. The armoured man whistled.

'Eyes off Kuro and back on me, worm. You and your friends caused a stir in the Broken Shield, I hear.'

'We caused nothing, sir,' said Trick, remembering to sound respectful. He had to charm this Gorgo, if such a thing were possible.

'Quit your lying right now. I'm Gorgo, the guild-master, see? There's nothing goes on in the docks that I don't know about, and that includes you and your poxy pals rocking up earlier today.'

'Master of what guild, my lord?'

The big man laughed, the belt of daggers rattling upon his metal hips.

'The Guild of Thieves, of course! Boarhammer

might control what happens above, but below ground, in the sewers, tunnels and warrens that riddle Sea Forge, I'm the boss. There ain't a crawl space I don't know about beneath this city. Pipes, worm! The latrines and drains of the poor and the rich – they're our means of getting everywhere. The Bog Baron, some have called me, but it cost 'em their tongues. If it's good enough for the rats, it's good enough for us. Me and my vermin have every square inch of Sea Forge mapped, above the cliffs and below, from the dunnies in the docks to the bath in Boarhammer's bedchamber. So, when I tell you to speak, you speak, right?'

Trick nodded as the guildmaster continued.

'You've got a hundred heartbeats to spill your story. If I don't like what I hear, Shiv and Clubb here will get to play with you . . .' His two henchmen chuckled, the bigger of the two licking his bulging lips.

Trick cleared his throat as the corpse continued to drift by. He'd never been one for stirring speeches. He looked around the room at the thieves. None of them appeared especially happy, their dour faces reflecting their grim lives. Trick's mind went back to the gates he'd seen, blocking the cliff road that led up to the city above. The germ of an idea was forming.

'My name is Trick Hope, sir. I'm not from Sea Forge – you can probably tell – and I'm certainly not here to cause any trouble with you. My beef's with Boarhammer up there,' he said, pointing upward.

'I've seen what he and his master have done to the Wildlands. You've heard of the village of Warriors Landing?' There were some grunts of recognition from the assembled thieves. 'Well, it's no more. Burned to the ground. Many butchered and those who remained have been enslaved. The Skull Army brought them here. They're destined for the arena. Entertainment for Boarhammer and his cronies.'

He saw some of them glancing at one another.

'Can you stand by and let that happen?' he continued. 'I know that it's just some village on the coast, but who's next? It won't be long until he starts trawling the docks for more "entertainment", believe you me.'

'There's already been folk disappearing,' said someone at the rear of the cavernous room. Gorgo glared over his shoulder and growled as Trick carried on.

'I saw those gates too, on the cliff road. That's your only way out of here, yeah? I can't imagine Boarhammer allows any of you guys to climb out of the mire. He wants to keep you where you are, where you know your place. You're at the bottom of the heap down here, just like everyone in the docks. It's the same everywhere – sewage rolls downhill, doesn't it? They're pooping on you, Boarhammer and his wealthy friends, from on high in Sea Forge city. He needs stopping. The Skull Army need stopping. Am I right? Who's with me?'

There was a chorus of muttering, even the nodding of heads, until Gorgo yelled angrily.

'Shut it, you lot! The worm's had his hundred heartbeats. We've heard what he has to say.'

Trick stared at Gorgo hopefully. The guildmaster stepped closer, his armour grating as he loomed over the boy.

'You come here, filling my lads' heads with stupid notions. Take on Boarhammer and the Skull Army? In this city? They *own* Sea Forge, worm. Ain't nothing happens in this city without Boarhammer's blessing. That was a good inn, the Broken Shield. Did a lot of business there, I did. Always a balancing act, keeping all those firecrackers, psychopaths and nutjobs in check under the one roof, but we managed, somehow. And you know what's happened since you and your pals caused your kerfuffle?'

Trick didn't answer. Gorgo continued.

'The Skull Army turned it over. Bagged what warriors they could – those they didn't kill or scare off – and dragged them away to fight in the arena. Then they put a torch to the place. It's rubble now. You've damaged my business, worm. Big time. And you have the gall to ask me to help you? You get my lads riled up looking for a fight, you're as good as putting the knife in 'em yourself. My lads know their place: by my side, down here, below ground.'

'But all those people the Skull Army has enslaved – you can help set them free! You have men, weapons. You know the city better than anyone, I reckon.' Trick looked at Gorgo imploringly. 'Please, show some kindness, Lord Gorgo. Some charity.'

The big man spat on the floor. 'Charity begins at home, worm.' He turned his back on Trick. 'Shiv! Clubb!' The two thugs who shadowed the guildmaster suddenly stepped forward, their faces lit up with ugly grins. 'Take him to Blood Beach and feed him to the carrion crabs. I don't want his body turning up.' He then addressed his gang. 'And, you lot, let this be a lesson. Any thoughts of uprising, of revolt, of taking the fight to Boarhammer up top, you'll face the same fate.'

Trick was about to beg for mercy, but the henchmen had him in their grasp. Within moments he was being dragged backwards into the darkness towards Blood Beach and the carrion crabs.

# CHAPTER TWENTY-TWO

'You don't have to do this, you know,' Trick said, as the two men bound his torso to a post beneath the jetty. The sand around his feet was littered with bones, many of which were recognizably human. 'You could always just let me go. Trust me, you'll never see me again.'

The rat-faced henchman, Shiv, grinned. 'We won't see you again this way either. Cheers all the same, but this is much more fun.'

His friend, Clubb, yanked the rope tight, causing Trick to wince. Not for the first time, Trick wished he was back home with his dad. Everything had gone to hell since they'd arrived in Sea Forge. First the fight in the tavern, then getting separated from Toki, Mungo, Kazumi and Zuma. Had they all been bagged by the Skull Army and shipped off to the arena? Were they to fight to the death for the amusement of Boarhammer?

And now here he was, tied to a rotten pillar under a pier in the night, about to be fed to carrion crabs, whatever they were. He was without friends or hope. All was lost.

'Seems a shame to leave him to the crabs, mind,' muttered Shiv. 'Would've been nice to cut him up a bit first.'

Clubb grunted in agreement as he shambled out from behind the post now that the boy was tied firmly in place. Shiv whipped a ragged length of cloth out of his pocket.

'Any last words?'

'Help!' screamed Trick, regretting it instantly as the thug punched him in the guts. He doubled up, hanging from his bonds, as the rat-faced thief tied the cloth round Trick's mouth, gagging him.

'That was a dumb last word, worm,' said the man, crouching down to pick up a pair of femurs from the sand. He struck them together, and the bones made a ringing sound like a glockenspiel. 'Dinner time, you horrible crustaceans!'

Trick lifted his chin and looked towards the sea. He saw shapes rising out of the brackish water beneath the pier, dark, barnacle-encrusted domes scuttling closer through the waves. There were three of them, each the size of an upturned wheelbarrow, their enormous pincers emerging from the foaming waves. By the moonlight he could see their twitching mandibles snapping together hungrily as they advanced up the beach towards their meal.

Shiv and Clubb were backing away, laughing, giddy with morbid excitement. Trick squealed, struggled, tried to shake loose the rope, but it was impossible. All the while the burbling chatter of the carrion crabs grew ever louder. They were less than three metres away now, all around the wooden posts as they closed on him.

'So long, worm,' said Shiv, turning to climb the stone wall of the docks. He took one step before something hit him from above. A shadowy figure landed on his shoulders and kicked him back down the beach. The rat-faced man flew, bouncing off the post beside Trick and hitting the sand, stunned. Clubb swung his fists at the assailant, but he was too slow as the other man darted beneath the flurry of blows. Trick looked back at the carrion crabs; the three of them were almost upon him now. He kicked out, striking Shiv on the head and making him holler in pain. One of the giant crabs turned towards the fallen thug, leaving two approaching the boy.

Clubb and his enemy were now locked in a vicious, spinning struggle. Clubb had managed to grab hold of the other man and refused to let go. He had him in his grasp now, squeezing hard and trying to crush the life from him. Trick saw the man well enough now: it was Kuro, the rogue who had seized him outside the Broken Shield. He was supposed to be with these men, wasn't he? And yet now he was fighting *against* them? Trick might have spent longer considering Kuro's change of allegiance if it hadn't been for the pressing business of the giant carnivorous crabs that were about to cut him to pieces.

Shiv screamed as the monster crab jumped on him, its pincers snapping as they went to work. He raised his hands, trying to shield his face from the beast, but his fingers were soon tumbling, chopped into tiny, bloody morsels. Trick turned back to the other two crabs. He kicked again, his boot connecting with one of the monsters as it attempted to slice into him. Another frantic kick sent the other briefly retreating, before it changed its angle of attack. One was coming from the left and one from the right; there was no way he could keep them both back.

Clubb held Kuro tightly as he attempted to crush him against the wall. Kuro's legs came up; he planted them firmly against the filthy stones and sprang backwards, launching the pair back down the beach. They landed in a heap, the wind knocked from Clubb as he relinquished his hold. Kuro wasted no time in rolling off the brute and dashing towards Trick. He jumped off the shell of the crab that was chopping up Shiv and landed behind the one nearest Trick. Seizing its shell, he strained, grunting, as he hurled it back to where Clubb lay. In a fluid motion, the ninja warrior withdrew his sword. The flashing blade severed both pincers of the third crab as it tried to grab Trick. The crab's mandibles yawned wide as it staggered clear, squirting inky blood across the grisly beach.

Then Kuro was behind Trick, sawing through the rope that bound him to the post. Trick collapsed forward, but Kuro caught him before he hit the sand and threw him over his shoulder, dancing between the wooden pier pillars as he made for the dock wall. They passed Clubb, wrestling in vain with a carrion crab as it turned his face into a hideous mask. Kuro accelerated, almost running up the stones, unhindered by the burden on his back. He landed with a thud on the docks, letting Trick slide off his shoulder, as they heard the dying cries of the two henchmen left behind on Blood Beach.

Trick wriggled clear as best he could, his hands still bound at his back, the gag still over his mouth. Kuro raised his hands.

'I'm not going to harm you, Trick Hope. I saved you for a reason. What you said down there, in the Thieves' Guild – did you mean it? You would help the disadvantaged, the weak and deprived of this city rise and topple Boarhammer?'

Trick nodded warily, his eyes narrow with suspicion.

'Then I shall help you, Trick Hope. Your quest is mine.' Kuro's face was hidden behind his mask, but Trick had to wonder if he was smiling, as his eyes twinkled under the light of the stars. 'Now let me help you with those bonds.'

Kuro moved a hand forward, but it never reached
Trick. A spear flew out of the night with expert, deadly
precision, striking his arm and pinning him to the
ground. He let out a shocked grunt, looking up and
around them, as did Trick. A figure stood on a rooftop
above them, silhouetted by the moon. A mane of long
blonde hair fluttered out from beneath the stranger's
domed helmet. Holding a shield in one hand, her other
hand moved to her sword, sliding it out of its scabbard
silently.

'Make another move, ninja, and it will be your last,'
said the woman, her voice deadly serious. 'The boy
is mine.'

# ERIKA'S SUMMONING

## England, AD 621

The young monk's prayers were silent, his crucifix clutched to his chest. He remained curled in a foetal position in the dust, rocking gently, fear gripping every nerve and sinew. Having just witnessed his defenceless brothers being butchered by a boatload of killers, he had no desire to climb out of his hidey-hole. The older priests hadn't run, hadn't hidden. They'd waited for the doors to be broken down, then stood there impassively as the invaders cut them down like cornstalks in the meadow. The youth had no such courage. His heart was filled with horror at what he'd witnessed, and what was to come.

Directly above he heard booted footsteps come to a halt. Dust was dislodged, finding its way through a gap in the floorboards and gently settling over his face. It was impossible to resist sneezing, but the monk stifled the sneeze and held his breath. A tiny squeak emerged and nothing more. He lay motionless, eyes turned upward, wondering whether the invaders had heard him. When the board was prised up and the helmeted face of a Viking raider appeared above him, he learned all he needed to know.

'What you got there?' came a voice from further away.

'Nothing,' replied the Viking, the voice lightly pitched.

'Let's have a look at nothing,' replied the other, yanking the helmeted raider aside. A big bearded brute with a gaping left eye socket stood there, a sick grin appearing in the nest of wiry hair.

'Don't look like nothing to me. Another dirty rat, eh? Smile for my axe, monk!'

He raised his axe, but his helmeted companion seized his wrist.

'Let this one go.'

'Why by Odin's sweetmeats would I do that?'

'He's just a child, Hagan. He hasn't even grown whiskers.'

'Nor shall he ever,' replied a third voice above. 'Cut him up, Hagan. Kill 'em all, says I!'

'Let go of my hand, Shield Maiden,' snarled Hagan, his beard bristling as his gap-toothed smile became a snarl. She kept her grip on the man's big forearm.

'You gone soft, girlie? You found these fools' God or something?'

'We should never have brought a girl with us on a raid, Hagan,' said the other man. 'I've said all along she's an ill omen. She's brought nothing but bad luck.'

'Last chance,' said the one they'd called Shield Maiden. 'Walk away now, nobody gets hurt. We've got all the gold we can carry and then some. Whaddaya say, Hagan?'

The bearded Viking suddenly spun, tearing his arm free to swipe his axe at her. It connected with her head, knocking off her helmet, which clattered to the floor. From the monk's hiding place below ground it was difficult for him to see what was happening, but he heard the unmistakable sound of steel upon shield followed by steel upon bone. There was a series of wet, crunching sounds, gurgles and death rattles, and then silence. Curiosity got the better of the young man and he lifted his head up through the floorboards.

The two men lay dead, and the woman picked up her battered helm from the ground. She stood before the altar in the apse, the stained-glass windows at her back, her long blonde hair falling about her shoulders. She could have been an angel.

'May God the Father watch over you, sweet lady,' whispered the boy, making the sign of the cross.

'There's only one Highfather, monk, and his name's Odin. And he'll be mad as hell when he sees what I've done to my uncle.'

She slammed her sword into its scabbard, adjusted her helmet and picked up her shield, just as the light through the stained glass intensified. The monk averted his gaze as she became a sliver of a silhouette, a heavenly blue light engulfing her. When he looked back she had gone, vanished into thin air.

'Angel,' whispered the young monk, taking hold of the floorboard and dragging it back into position as he returned to the safety of his hiding place.

# CHAPTER TWENTY-THREE

Kuro didn't have time to answer the woman on the rooftop. Before he could speak, another figure emerged from the shadows on the docks, one Trick recognized.

'You want the boy,' said Kazumi, addressing the woman above and raising her naginata as she prowled forward, 'you have to beat me first.'

'As you wish,' said the blonde stranger, sliding down the tiled roof before leaping to the street below. She wore a leather cuirass over her body, and held her sword and shield raised before her with expert ease. Her blue eyes flitted from the ninja on the dock to the samurai standing nearby, sizing up each of her opponents. All the while, Trick squirmed on the ground, trying to work his hands loose from his bonds. If he could have cried out, he would have.

Kuro pulled the spear from his arm – it came free

from the black fabric, having narrowly missed the flesh. In the same breath it flew from his wrist towards the blonde woman, whose quickly raised shield deflected it in the direction of Kazumi. She swung her naginata, striking the spear out of the air and sending it skittering across the dock. Kuro stood over Trick now, his own sword in hand as he glared at the two women.

'The boy is in my custody,' said the ninja. 'I do not wish to kill either of you, but if you press me . . .'

'Brave words,' said Kazumi. 'He came to Sea Forge with me and he'll leave with me. If either of you stands in my way you'll never see the sunrise.'

The blonde woman suddenly sprang forward. 'Sweet Odin but you two *talk* too much!'

Her longsword struck Kazumi's naginata, but the samurai parried with ease. This prompted Kuro to attack, and three throwing stars whistled towards her. Her shield went up, catching all three of them. She struck the back of the shield with the fist that held her sword, dislodging the shuriken and sending them flying back at the ninja. He leapt, rolling clear as they clattered around Trick.

The boy rolled as the three warriors went at one another, trading blows with katana, longsword and naginata. Trick found one of the stars on the dock, picked it up with shaking fingertips and turned it against his bonds. He began to cut the rope, his eyes fixed upon the duelling fighters. If he could, he would help Kazumi, as she was the only one among them he trusted. As for Kuro – the idea of helping the poor of the city had struck a chord with the ninja. Perhaps he *could* be of use to them. But the blonde woman? Trick had figured her out now. The fair complexion, the distinctive shield and the Odin curse: this was the Shield Maiden Toki had mentioned. Whether she was honourable or not was another matter.

The rope came loose, allowing Trick to leap to his feet. He tugged the gag loose and dashed towards the battling trio.

'Stop it!' he shouted. 'Quit fighting each other!'

He rushed in, trying to grab Kazumi. It was no good. She was completely committed to the fight, slashing, parrying and counter-attacking in turn with her naginata. She threw an elbow back, catching Trick in the shoulder as she barged him clear of the melee. He flew across the dock, crashing into a barrel and a stack of lobster pots. They clattered down around him as the battle raged on.

'How's tricks, Trick?'

He looked up. There, perched upon a lantern post, was a familiar big black bird.

'Kaw!' he exclaimed, relieved to see the pesky crow again. The bird was looking over the dock's edge to the beach, where more carrion crabs had joined the others at the banquet.

'Made a bit of a mess down there, didn't you, kid? Still, better them than you, eh?'

'You have to help me, Kaw,' said Trick, struggling wearily to his feet. 'You've gotta make them stop. They're going to kill each other!'

'The three amigos? No chance, pal. Ain't getting my feathers ruffled in that scrap. I'm likely to end up as a crow kebab! I'm afraid it's down to you, Trick. You're the leader of this gang, you're the Black Moon Warrior. It's *you* who needs to tear them apart.'

Trick glowered at the crow. 'Remind me again what purpose you serve?'

Trick left the bird, and stalked cautiously towards the combatants. All three were masters of their weapons and individual fighting styles. Kazumi was all grace, her elegant sweeping moves kept her foes at bay with the naginata and she chose her moments to strike carefully. The Shield Maiden was the opposite, all strength and fury, trusting her armour and shield to protect her should any blade find its way past her longsword. Kuro's movements were all speed and stealth, he faded in and out of the fight, striking quickly and quietly. Trick had to choose which of the three he would try to distract without getting hurt, let alone killed. His shoulder still throbbed from where Kazumi had struck him.

He decided on Kuro eventually. The ninja kept disengaging, affording Trick the chance to dive in and try to catch his attention. He darted forward and instantly regretted his rash and foolish move.

The ninja suddenly sprang high, just as the Shield

Maiden was lunging at him. The longsword cut through the air, straight through the spot Kuro had occupied and on towards Trick. He gasped as the blade zoomed towards his head. He let instinct, and the nerve and agility that had carried him across rooftops back home, take over. His hips slid, torso twisting, head falling to one side as the Viking's sword thrust by. He felt the steel's razor edge kiss his cheek, slicing open the flesh as, loose-limbed and dizzy, he collapsed.

His head struck a paving stone with a sickening crack. The three warriors stood over him, their fight finished, the stars twinkling overhead. The last thing Trick heard was a crow's caw as the darkness engulfed him.

# CHAPTER TWENTY-FOUR

When Trick awoke, he felt like somebody had used his head for a football. There was a stabbing pain behind his eyes, as if a knitting needle had been shoved up his nostril and scrambled his brains. The left-hand side of his face felt feverishly hot, while the right was as cold as ice.

If he could have gone back to sleep he would have, but that seemed impossible with the drums that banged in his skull. Trick wasn't remotely interested in alcohol – the closest he'd come was a sip of Grandpa's Guinness one Christmas, which had been vile – but he imagined that this was what a hangover must feel like. His eyes slowly focused.

'You're not dead then,' said Kalaban. 'That's something we can be thankful for.'

'Kalaban!' exclaimed Trick happily, instantly regretting

it as a thousand bottles seemed to shatter in his head. He winced as he struggled upright in his bed. To Trick's surprise, there was no sign of the old man. Only Kaw sat on the foot of his bed, his head cocked to one side.

'Where are you, Kalaban?'

'I'm here, in a fashion,' replied the old man, but Trick realized that the voice was coming from Kaw. The bird's eyes were pale and white, as if he were possessed by a spirit. In a way, he was.

'How are you *doing* that?' whispered Trick in amazement.

'This is how I stay in touch with you, Trick: via Kaw.' The beak snapped as the bird spoke. 'Should I need to speak to you, I do it through my black-feathered familiar. I can only be brief, though. This will exhaust my little friend – and me for that matter.'

'Where am I?'

'You're in a friend's home,' came Kalaban's reply. They were in the burnt-out attic of a tower, blackened timbers providing them with shelter from the elements. Just beyond Kaw there was open space, and the docklands were visible below where the floorboards splintered away into nothing. In the recesses of the fire-damaged loft, another figure moved in the shadows.

'In Sea Forge? I don't *have* any friends here.'

'You have one,' said the figure, stepping forward. It was the man in black.

'Kuro,' said Kalaban through the crow. 'Be a good fellow and tell the others he's awake. We'll be down to join you forthwith.'

The ninja faded back into the shadows, leaving the black bird and the schoolboy alone.

'This is Kuro's tower?'

'He's claimed it as his own. The fact that the locals believe it is haunted means you're quite safe here. Nobody will come knocking.'

Kaw hopped up the bed and on to Trick's chest, tilting his head once more as he examined the cut on the boy's cheek. His white eyes seemed to stare straight through Trick.

'The wound will heal, in time. You'll have quite a scar too. It was your head hitting the flags that caused the most damage. You've been unconscious for well over a day.'

'A day? How the heck did the fight end without them killing each other?'

'Seems they were interested in hearing what a talking crow had to say,' replied Kalaban, as the bird he possessed shook its feathers. 'Kaw speaking up grabbed their attention. You've our feathered friend to thank for intervening.'

Trick shook his head, causing Kaw to flap before settling. 'It all went wrong when we got here, Kalaban. I lost Toki, Mungo and Zuma at the Broken Shield Inn.

It's a miracle Kazumi found me again. I've made such a mess of things.'

'What nonsense,' said the hermit. 'You've misplaced your friends, that is all, and made new ones in the meantime. Kuro is the greatest ninja ever to have entered the Wildlands. His exploits are legendary. How he fell into the employment of Gorgo baffles me. And the Shield Maiden remains close by, desiring to speak with you. No, you have powerful allies, Trick Hope. Lose one, gain another – you are never without.'

'But what of the other three?'

'Toki and Mungo have been taken to Boarhammer's arena, so far as we can tell,' said the possessed bird, craning his neck as if looking out of the fractured roof. Trick followed Kaw's blind gaze. The gladiatorial palace was visible, the sun shining bright above the cliffs, casting half the docks below into shadow.

'We saw the arena in Mudflatt. That's where we met Zuma.'

'Oh no, this is nothing like the pit in the shanty port. Boarhammer's arena is legendary. It's a temple to death and despair, and the wealthy and well-to-do of Sea Forge flock there for excitement. Peasants provide mild entertainment when thrown to Boarhammer's beasts, but it's the warriors who provide the true spectacle. This is a common occurrence. Your friends aren't the first and they won't be the last.'

Trick shivered, despite the heat of the midday sun.

'No. When the Skull Army arrived at the Broken Shield, they dragged away some suitable participants before shutting the place down. By which I mean killing the landlord, his family, his pet dog and then putting the place to the torch. Your feisty friends, along with many other luckless warriors, are now destined for the arena. Perhaps you need to stop Boarhammer before this event, Trick?'

Trick sighed. 'I am *trying*, Kalaban. Believe me! This whole quest business isn't easy, you know?'

'I know, my young friend, I know. I found that myself when I first faced Boneshaker, but there's simply no other way. You're the Wildlands' only hope. How are you progressing with the other two parts of your quest?'

'Let me think,' said Trick sarcastically, tapping a finger on his chin. 'Well, let's see. We went to the Broken Shield Inn searching for warriors, and managed to get my party disbanded and the inn burned down. So I reckon I fluffed that bit. And, as for Ravenblade, I'm looking for a needle in a haystack there. I've got sod all chance of finding that flipping thing.'

The crow hopped back to the foot of the bed. 'Stay strong, Trick. You may feel that all is lost, but, trust me – you've made progress.'

Trick nodded but he really didn't see it. He felt hopelessly out of his depth. The idea of leading an offensive against Boneshaker terrified him. The title of

Black Moon Warrior sat uneasily on his shoulders. He changed the subject.

'You didn't mention Zuma. What happened to him?'

'No sign of the Jaguar Warrior. He disappeared during the melee in the inn. Kazumi didn't see him carted away by the Skull Army. She is convinced that he's disappeared with that strongbox of money and you're unlikely to see him again. We'll have to see what happens.'

Trick sat up in bed, throwing his legs out and pulling on his boots. He felt rough beyond description, but lying in bed was getting nothing done. From his lofty perch, he could hear the clashing of weapons below. Immediately, Trick felt anxiety rise.

'Sounds like a fight.'

'That, Trick Hope, is your companions in training.'

'Toki, Mungo and Kazumi,' said Trick, pulling his boots on. 'Zuma and Kuro . . . I must say, you seem very well informed, considering we left you back in your cave at Tangle Falls, old man. How do you know so much?'

The crow ruffled his feathers. 'Kaw acts as my eyes and ears over great distances. And I've been in Sea Forge for a number of days, courtesy of my familiar. From the rooftops, we even found time to play the part of a crazy old prophet in Speaker's Square, providing a voice of opposition to Boneshaker.'

'That was you? The mad old bloke shouting about the Black Moon Warrior?'

The crow chuckled. 'I was here three days before you. Then it was simply a case of starting the rumour of your impending arrival. Kaw has been a busy bird. He's been hopping over rooftops, shouting into streets and calling through open windows. A disembodied voice can travel great distances – you'd be amazed how many people have now heard of the Black Moon Warrior. Sometimes fate needs a helping hand, and hearsay is a powerful weapon. We sow these tiny seeds, and over time oaks shall grow.'

Trick admired the old man's cunning. Still, he felt sick that he'd made such a mess of things. 'I lost everything, you know? My staff, my bag – it had the map in it, and other stuff, besides.'

Kaw squawked and hopped to one side of the bed end, revealing a chair in the corner of the room. There was the schoolbag and Trick's quarterstaff. 'You're very absent-minded, Trick Hope. If you're not losing warriors you're losing your belongings. Just as well Kazumi can think on her feet, eh? Oh, and I noticed you have a passenger in there too. Don't worry, Kaw found a couple of juicy bluebottles to feed him. Provided quite a meal, apparently.'

Trick grinned. 'You found Sparky?'

'That's what you've called him?' chuckled the bird.

'Seemed an appropriate name. Thanks, Kalaban. Will you remain with us, then?'

'Sadly, no,' said the bird, straightening his back stiffly.

'As I said, I cannot stay in this feathered vessel for long. Kaw will be wanting his body back. And I must remain at Tangle Falls, out of sight. Were I to reveal myself entirely to any of Boneshaker's minions, it would bring the Dark Lord's fury down upon us. He would focus all his efforts on crushing you before your quest has truly begun. I must remain invisible for as long as possible – stick to the shadows. Let Boneshaker think me dead. That would be best for everyone. You may then cross the Wildlands without additional complications from the Skull Army. Well, no more than any gang of heroes would encounter, anyway. If the time is right for me to reveal myself I shall, but only when it will best serve your cause.'

'My cause?'

'You still want to go home, don't you?'

Trick nodded.

'And one last matter,' said the disembodied hermit. 'You said you'd investigated the Broken Shield Inn. I find that hard to believe – you were only there long enough to start a bar brawl.'

Trick opened his mouth to object, but the wise man continued.

'I recommend that you return there.'

'But the warriors have all been seized by Boar-hammer's men. What's the point?'

'Have you retrieved Ravenblade?' Trick shook his head as the bird continued. 'Leave no stone unturned, even if it's burnt rubble. Understand? I said you'd find answers there, and I never lie.'

'But I looked, Kalaban . . .'

'Then look again. Don't give up so easily. Remember, when your chin hits your chest, lift it – look up. Seek and you shall find.'

The boy nodded, irked by the riddling talk.

'Good,' said the crow, suddenly looking a little uneasy on his perch. 'Well, until next time, Trick Hope.'

Then the bird keeled over, landing on his back at the end of the bed, feet in the air like a comedic dead parrot. Kaw blinked, the white mist fading from his eyes as the familiar beady black returned. The crow trembled, rolling on to his belly, wings akimbo, and he snapped his beak wearily as he spoke.

'I hate it when he does that.'

# CHAPTER TWENTY-FIVE

'You're sure it's wise to include him?' asked Erika, the Shield Maiden.

'Kuro's got an axe to grind, or a katana, I should say,' replied Trick, watching his pet lightning grub crawl across his hand. The insect's abdomen was toughening up on its diet of flies, its bioluminescence invisible in the sunlight. It really was a whopper compared to the glow-worms he'd found back home. A short distance away, Kuro put Kazumi through her paces. 'And, besides, he's letting us use his home. I'd say that's pretty cool of him.'

Trick and the Viking sat on the steps of the ninja's ruined tower, the tall walls of the courtyard protecting them from prying eyes. Kuro had cut his ties with the Thieves' Guild after the incident at Blood Beach and his switch to Trick's side. His tumbledown tower and its grounds were the perfect base for the group as they prepared for the coming battle. A single ivy-choked gate provided an entrance to the ruins, though this was invisible to an untrained eye. Kuro was a very clever fellow, it transpired, having picked a home that was unwelcoming and forbidding. Its grim appearance and the rumoured resident ghosts kept the locals away.

'Why trust him?' asked the Shield Maiden.

'He saved me on Blood Beach when they were feeding me to the carrion crabs. That makes him an OK guy in my eyes.'

'But what's his angle?'

'His beef is with Boarhammer, apparently. He wants the warlord dead in revenge for all the crimes he's committed in Sea Forge, some against Kuro's best mates. Revenge is as good a reason as any, I guess.'

'We *all* want revenge against Boarhammer,' replied Erika. 'Some more than others.'

'Kuro says the warlord is unreachable. The only time you can get near him is at the arena, and even then it's almost impossible. Says he has a balcony on top of a giant wooden viewing tower from which he watches the contests.'

'Nobody is unreachable, boy,' said the Viking, grimly. 'I would question the loyalty of one who used to belong to the Thieves' Guild, though.'

Trick turned to Erika. 'You said it yourself: "used to be". You fought for Boarhammer in the arena too, didn't you? Guess you all have your shady pasts.'

'I was a captive gladiator. I had to win Boarhammer's trust before seizing my moment to break out of there. Many people died at my hand in the dust of the arena. When I escaped, I was the champion, beloved by all those infantile idiots who pander to the warlord's whims. That's why he has a bounty on my head. Kuro worked for Gorgo by choice. Big difference, child.'

'If you don't quit calling me "boy" and "child", you and I are gonna have a falling out,' said Trick, clearly annoyed by Erika's patronizing manner. She was taken aback. 'And, besides, you've joined us and I know very little about you, Erika. Do we reconsider your allegiance?'

She laughed. 'Allegiance? You arrived in Sea Forge with one of my brethren in tow. It's fair to say you caused one hell of a ruckus in the Broken Shield Inn. That's when you came to my attention. A boy, a Viking and a gaggle of sell-swords? I needed to know what my kinsman was doing taking orders from a lad who can't even grow whiskers on his chin. I want to speak with Toki, discover what he knows from the homeland, and whether he has encountered other Norsemen in the Wildlands.

'I hear that my people have been banding together in this world, seeking one another out, just as you see Kuro and Kazumi forming bonds before us now. There is something to be said for being with one's own kind. I seek my kin, Trick Hope, not friendship with you and your motley gang of fools.'

Trick nodded as the lightning bug crept across his knuckles. 'So you're with us until we get Toki back. Fine, but I warn you – he's with me.'

'With you? You're some mongrel from the land of Angles. Why in Valhalla would Toki choose you over me?'

'You wouldn't understand,' said Trick, opening his schoolbag to pop the insect back into its makeshift nest. 'It's a brother thing.'

That left Erika bemused and speechless, which suited Trick fine as he hid his grin. Toki had been a good friend, and the vow they'd made to each other had only grown stronger with time. He wanted the young Viking back by his side, sooner rather than later, and this crazy Shield Maiden would help him achieve that.

They had spent the last two days preparing for the arena's grand event tomorrow. This involved Kazumi, Kuro and Erika learning one another's moves and fighting styles, and working out how they complemented each other. Erika passed on all she knew about the arena, in particular where Boarhammer would sit once the 'games' commenced.

The grand viewing platform was the Lord of Sea Forge's chosen spot, overlooking the entire arena and granting him and his cronies the best view of the mayhem below. Throughout this hectic period, Kazumi also trained Trick in fighting with his quarterstaff, passing on her knowledge. Indeed, each of the warriors took the time to help him to build his confidence. The road to becoming a warrior was clearly long, arduous and full of bruised knuckles and kneecaps.

'Ladies and gentlemen, the wanderer has returned!'

The warriors ceased sparring and Trick and Erika turned towards the gate. Zuma had materialized through the vine-strangled gate, strolling along without a care in the world. Of the strongbox he'd last been seen with there was no sign. Kazumi sprang towards the gatehouse, naginata raised and ready to strike. The Jaguar Warrior leapt clear of where she landed and prepared himself for a fight, his macuahuitl raised, studded shards of black glass ready to puncture flesh.

'Pack it in, Kazumi,' shouted Trick as everyone rushed towards them.

'Hack him in, more like!' she replied, twirling her naginata as she and Zuma circled one another. 'You dare return to us – so late in the day – with our companions gone and our money vanished?'

'In my defence,' said Zuma, 'that strongbox was never yours.'

'And I see you no longer have it with you.'

'Indeed. I gorged myself on the handful of coppers and silvers that were left within.'

'There was *gold* in that box, Aztec!'

'It was loose change, samurai. The gold was spent on the ferry, or have you conveniently forgotten that?'

'So you come crawling back to us, seeking to rejoin us and get your grubby hands on more gold?'

'Forget your coins,' said Kuro, slowly raising his katana. 'How did you find your way into my tower? How did you know your friends were here as my guests?'

Zuma took one look at the tumbledown tower and weed-covered courtyard. 'Guests? Your idea of hospitality is not the same as mine, ninja. Lady Kazumi snores like a pregnant hog. I would've heard her from Mudfla–'

The samurai's naginata slashed at the Jaguar Warrior's throat, but he leaned back and it clattered aside. He lunged and Kazumi brought the stave of her weapon up to deflect the blow. Erika and Kuro watched, ready to jump in.

'Stop it!' roared Trick, making them cease instantly. They looked at him, panting like rabid dogs. 'Can we stop the accusations? And the attempts at killing each other? Let's hear what Zuma has to say!'

'And if we don't like what he says?' asked Kazumi.

'He's walked in here alone, facing possible death. His reason must be pretty good.' Trick turned to Zuma. 'Go ahead, mate. Say your piece. And you'd better make it good.'

The scolded samurai stepped away, glowering, her simmering glare fixed upon the Jaguar Warrior as he thanked Trick for his kind words.

'Contrary to what our hot-headed friend is saying,

I haven't been frittering away our funds,' said Zuma, turning his back on Kazumi. 'After the brawl at the Broken Shield Inn, I made for the gatehouse on the cliffs. With the money we had left, I paid for passage to the Upper City.'

'You didn't think it'd be best to consult us first?' asked Trick.

'There was hardly an "us" to consult,' replied the Aztec. 'We were separated like chaff on the wind. Believe me, it would've been easy to forge on and seek further fortune alone, but I gave my word to you, Trick Hope. I'll fight by your side, but I'll take the lion's share of any gold we find.'

'You mean the jaguar's share?' said Erika. He continued, ignoring the Shield Maiden.

'I've been in the Upper City since then. Merchants, bankers, slavers and spice merchants – they run Sea Forge from on high, all with Boarhammer's say-so. It's a world away from this dungheap.' He looked around at the ruins that the group had made their base.

'Remember, this is my home,' grunted Kuro. 'Mind what you say, stranger.'

'Or what?' asked Zuma. 'You want to dance, wait your turn. I think the samurai is next.'

Trick clapped his hands. 'Good God, can you all quit for a moment! You're like kids at times! If you can save the posturing and duels until *after* we've freed the city, that would be tickety-boo. Now, Zuma, you were saying . . .?'

The Aztec's smile was cocky and confident. He clearly enjoyed taking centre stage.

'There's a big event on its way – the whole of the Upper City is talking about it. The warriors who were captured during the raid on the Broken Shield – I count Mungo and Toki in that luckless band – await their moment of glory in two days' time.'

'Two days?'

'Boarhammer's putting on a grand show, a spectacle to honour Boneshaker. That's why he's enslaved so many opponents and scooped up any warriors he can find. Those poor souls you mentioned from Warriors Landing will all be put to sword in the arena, in one way or another. A bloody day approaches . . .'

'All those warriors, in one place,' muttered Trick, ideas taking shape in his mind.

'Also, Boarhammer recently had a special guest staying at his palace. An envoy from Boneshaker.'

'Envoy?' asked Trick.

'He arrived a week ago accompanied by an elite group of the Skull Army called the Blackguard. They were delivering your friends from Warriors Landing. This envoy, you couldn't miss him. Big guy with a full helm.'

'They like their full helms, don't they?' said Erika, managing a chuckle.

'They do indeed,' smiled Zuma. 'Only this one's is adorned with antlers. Looks like a devil, and they call him –'

'Tombstone.' Trick finished Zuma's news for him.

'You know of him?' asked Zuma.

Trick nodded, recalling his encounter with the giant warlord in Warriors Landing. 'He's a monster.'

'What kind of name's that?' added Kuro. 'Tombstone?'

'Probably earned by the number of bodies he's put in the ground,' replied the Aztec.

'Boneshaker's lieutenants visited Boarhammer when I used to fight in the arena,' said Erika. 'Don't ever remember meeting a Tombstone.'

'You were too busy lying face down in the sand,' said Zuma.

'So, what?' said Trick. 'Tombstone was just here to drop off prisoners for the arena? He didn't strike me as a gopher.'

'Gopher?' they all said in unison.

'A lackey, a fetcher, a runner. Tombstone is Boneshaker's right hand, so Kalaban said.'

'The boy's correct,' said Zuma. 'He was the toast of the Upper City. I've heard plenty about him from those fools and fops who lick Boarhammer's behind. Tombstone's also known as the Lord of Chaos, just as likely to kill his own men in battle when the madness seizes him. He'll stoop to any dirty trick in order to win the fight.'

'Sounds like you two would get along,' said Kazumi. Zuma simply grinned at her.

'So it was a big deal then?' said Erika. 'But now he's gone?'

'He was delivering instructions to the Lord of Sea Forge,' said the Jaguar Warrior, everyone now hanging on his words. 'There's something in this city that Boneshaker wants badly – a weapon of some sort. Boarhammer's job is to find it, and quickly. He'll turn the city upside down in the process, from the docks upward. That's why the Broken Shield Inn was turned over and burned – our fracas was just an excuse. Those soldiers were already *there*, in the docks. Rumour has it that the Broken Shield was top of the list for them to hit. Who knows why . . .'

Trick didn't react, but his mind was whirring. Seeking a weapon? In Sea Forge? He had to mean Ravenblade, the elusive sword that Trick had failed to find. Kalaban had said already that Trick would have to return to the torched inn and dig for answers; he'd been putting it off, worried about leaving the relative safety of Kuro's tower, but he could hide no longer.

Trick felt the spark of an idea form in his head. It was time for him to get back there, but there was another pressing port of call, far more dangerous than rummaging around in a pile of charcoal and cinders. He turned and looked back at his companions sizing one another up, their alliance still uneasy, especially since the unexpected return of the Jaguar Warrior.

They'd continued their conversation while Trick had been lost in thought.

'But we're only a handful,' said Kazumi. 'How can we get close to Boarhammer when we're stuck down here in the poor quarter?'

'And that gate only works one way,' added Erika. 'It was easy enough for Zuma to come through it, but he can't return to the Upper City now. No, the cliff road is closed to us. There is no other way to reach the arena.'

'Kuro,' said Trick quietly, drawing the ninja away from the others.

'What is it, Master Hope?'

'You think you can get me back into the Broken Shield without being seen?'

'Not a problem, but I warn you now: it's a smouldering ruin.'

'I get that,' said Trick. 'And another thing. I need to go back to the Thieves' Guild.'

'Are you insane? Why would you wish to return there?'

Trick's smile was cocksure, but it hid the rising tide of nerves. 'I seek an audience with Gorgo.'

# CHAPTER TWENTY-SIX

'Tell me again why we're here,' said Kuro, staring up at the burnt, blackened rafters of the Broken Shield Inn. The stars sparkled beyond the exposed roof, a blanket of blinking diamonds.

'I'm looking for a sword.'

'You should have said; I've a rack of them in my armoury.'

Trick stepped gingerly through the rubble, a hooded lantern held before him, casting a roving spotlight across the ground. The lamp was invaluable; he'd grabbed it from the ninja's tower and its controlled beam allowed them to search the ruined tavern without drawing attention. Trick was light on his feet, but more than once the floor beneath him gave way, scorched timbers collapsing or pitted bricks crumbling. The Skull Army had really gone to town on the place.

'You should have asked the others to join us,' said the ninja. 'Many hands make light work.'

'I'm not sure where I stand on Erika and Zuma. Can't say I entirely trust them yet. Kazumi? Sure. That's why I've left her at your tower, to keep an eye on the other two. And, besides, you and I are going somewhere else tonight, remember?'

'Gorgo,' said the man in black, his voice a whisper.

Trick looked back into the shadows. He couldn't see the ninja, but he knew he was there. Erika had questioned whether the man could be trusted. Trick had no such concerns. Kuro had proved himself when he'd saved Trick from Gorgo's thugs at Blood Beach, effectively destroying any ties he had with the Thieves' Guild. Since then he'd offered Trick and his companions his home, and sworn his katana to the boy's cause.

'You never did say why you took my side,' said Trick, his voice low as he continued his search.

'Yours seemed a good fight,' came the disembodied reply. 'My business with Gorgo had run its course.'

'How so?'

'When I arrived in Sea Forge, I had nobody – no friends, no allies. My reputation meant nothing here either – my name was built back in Japan, a legend carved in blood. But that man is gone now, the old Kuro replaced by someone different.'

'I don't follow.'

Kuro disengaged from the darkness now, materializing by Trick's side as he helped him sift through the wreckage of the inn. He effortlessly lifted a marble bar top, shifting it to one side as the two left no stone unturned. The job was huge, and they'd already been there for almost an hour.

'In Japan, I was a paid killer, a blade for hire. I worked for the highest bidder, the warlord who could afford my fee. My life was good. I wanted for nothing, and I cared nought for those who died at my hand. Sword, poison, arrow or shuriken – there were many tools of my trade.'

Trick shivered. The man was a stone-cold killing machine. He was a flipping ninja, for goodness' sake, and unless the boy was mistaken he was also now his mate. Trick's life just kept getting weirder.

'What changed?'

Kuro shrugged. 'Expectations, I suppose. I only ever had one job in Japan: to kill my master's enemies. Killing was the only language I understood, and I never questioned it. Arriving in the Wildlands turned my world upside down. When I got to Sea Forge, I fell in with what I thought I knew. I offered my katana to Gorgo for work, and for a while life felt close to normal for me. And then I saw the injustice was no different in Gorgo's company: the poor being crushed by the powerful, the greedy getting fatter – principally the guildmaster. The majority of the thieves in his employ live in fear of what he'll do to them. You probably sensed it when you first met him, in the sewers. Even thieves deserve a better life than the one Gorgo allows them. When you turned up, I realized I had a choice.'

'A choice?'

'Free will. I'd never considered it before.' The ninja stopped what he was doing, placing a black-gloved hand on Trick's shoulder. He gave it a squeeze. 'I may have been an assassin back in my own world and time, but here I've found something more: a cause, a purpose. I fight for you, Trick Hope.'

Trick smiled, overwhelmed by the man's words. 'Thanks, Kuro. Knowing you're fighting *alongside* me and not *against* me is wicked.'

'Wicked?'

'Trust me, mate,' said Trick, patting the man's hand before returning to his search. 'Wicked's a good thing on this occasion.'

Having the ninja on his side made Trick feel good in a way he couldn't explain. The man was clearly older than Toki, younger than Kalaban, saner than Mungo and not as wild as Zuma. He was strong but controlled, thoughtful and powerful. Trick suddenly realized who the ninja reminded him of; it was his father, Malcolm Hope. Not for the last time, the pangs of homesickness tugged at his innards, his heart aching for a reunion with his old man. With no father-figure in this world of warriors, Kuro appeared to be the next best thing.

'So, this sword,' said the ninja. 'What does it look like?'

Trick grabbed the pendant hanging round his neck between two grubby, soot-stained fingers. 'It's made from the same black glass as this.'

'A glass sword? Sounds fragile.'

'You'd think, huh? Kalaban says it's uber-powerful. Used to belong to Boneshaker, and that's why he's got Tombstone and Boarhammer looking for it.'

'Perhaps they found it when they turned the place over, Master Hope?'

'Maybe. But the old hermit told me to come and look again, so here I am. Reckon they never found it.'

'Perhaps it was never here at all?'

Trick continued his search, heading back through the ruined inn towards the front entrance. It was hopeless. The parts of the building that still stood threatened to collapse at any moment, and the debris underfoot was an indiscriminate mass of black rubble.

'Perhaps it's meant to remain hidden, Master Hope? I know how the myths of my homeland work. Powerful items tend to be found by powerful individuals. Maybe you aren't destined to find this sword.'

'That'd suit me fine,' said Trick with a sigh as they arrived back at the door. He closed the shutter on the hooded lantern as they neared the street, concealing their presence. 'I never wanted to be part of some dumb prophecy anyway. I'd much rather someone else turned out to be the Black Moon Warrior.'

'You've looked, Master Hope. That's all you could have done. The sword isn't here. If it was, you would have found a clue,' said the ninja, stalking out of the ruined inn.

Trick kicked at the rubble, sending a chunk of burnt brick skittering. Kalaban had told him not to quit, but what else had the riddling hermit said? The hairs on Trick's neck were suddenly all aquiver. *When your chin hits your chest, lift it – look up.* Trick did that, his eyes searching the ruined walls of the tavern.

'There would have been a sign of some kind,' said Kuro.

Trick stopped dead in his tracks, hit by a lightning bolt of inspiration. A sign. He lifted the shutter on the lantern once more, letting an iris of light slowly shimmer into life.

'Master Hope,' whispered Kuro, dancing back up the steps towards the boy. 'The light!'

'Hush a mo,' said Trick, tilting the lantern and letting its beam wander up the demolished walls round the doorway. It weaved over the scorched stones before rising higher, finally settling on the creaking shield that swung from its rusting chains above the door, one of the few fixtures to have remained untouched by the fire that had ravaged the inn.

Kuro chuckled with realization. 'By the gods . . .'

The lantern light lingered over the tarnished black blade, buried deep in the filthy timbers of the sundered shield. The handle, unnoticed on Trick's previous visit, drew his eye this time. It was fashioned in the shape of a bird's head, sharp beak at right angles to the cross guard, all carved from polished black glass.

'We have our sign,' Trick said with a smile. 'And we have our sword.'

# CHAPTER TWENTY-SEVEN

'You sure you know what you're doing?' whispered Kuro, back to back with Trick as the smoke bomb cleared. Ravenblade remained holstered across the ninja's shoulder, swaddled in wraps, its blade crossed with his katana.

'Absolutely,' the boy lied, holding his quarterstaff up before him as the confused mob of thieves encircled them.

The ninja had been able to lead him right into the heart of the guildmaster's kingdom, sneaking silently past sentries and sidestepping patrols. Trick was a sure-footed and agile young man, but in the presence of Kuro he felt like a noisy, mouth-breathing, bumbling klutz. The ninja was like a ghost, sliding in and out of shadows and vanishing from view. It took all Trick's concentration and guile to keep his eyes focused on his companion in the darkness – and more than once he disappeared entirely from view, only to reappear at the boy's side.

With Gorgo's guards dodged, Kuro had managed to reach the old catacomb cavern, revealing his and Trick's presence in dramatic fashion. The smoke grenade was an evasion weapon for the ninja; this was the first time he'd used one to make a grand entrance.

'Well, well, well,' said Gorgo, tossing a half-eaten chicken leg into one of the channels that ran through the stone chamber. His men parted to allow him through, and the guildmaster wiped his greasy fingers on his shining steel breastplate. 'I never thought I'd see this. The worm returns, as does the traitorous scumbag who killed Shiv and Clubb at Blood Beach.'

'It was the carrion crabs that killed them,' said Kuro.

'You helped them though, didn't you, ninja? You come back to rob me? As a once-trusted lieutenant you know many of my secrets, Kuro. I'm looking forward to killing you. I may even break out a new knife for you.'

'It doesn't have to be like this,' said the man in black, his voice calm. 'Hear the boy out.'

'I heard what he had to say last time, and it didn't interest me then. Bowmen!'

A number of thieves darted forward through the ranks, crossbows raised and levelled at the two intruders.

'I have a challenge for you, Gorgo,' shouted Trick, his voice breaking as he cried out.

'Ha! I don't need to accept *any* challenge, especially not one from a worm.'

'You're not afraid of a kid, are you?'

A murmur rumbled through the crowd and Gorgo noted it. He turned back to Trick.

'What's this challenge?'

'You say you can kill me,' said Trick, 'and that's probably true. But at least give me a chance to face you in combat. Let me die fighting.'

Gorgo guffawed. 'I can do that.'

'Oh,' said the boy, 'and one more thing. If I win, your men are free to join my cause.'

There was a frisson of nervous excitement in the Thieves' Guild throne room. 'Shut up, you shower!' yelled Gorgo, who clearly dominated every soul in the room. 'You lot swore an oath to me. I own you, and all your poxy debts!'

None would meet his gaze, the cowed thieves averting their eyes from their boss's stare. He turned slowly back to Trick, an enormous grin filling his face.

'Right, worm. Let's do this. I promise you, it won't be quick. Take a moment first, if you wish,' he chuckled, as his men gathered round him, fussing and flattering him.

Trick and Kuro were alone, although a dozen crossbows remained trained on them. Trick saw the ninja's eyes dart from man to man.

'Some of these are good men. I'd hate to kill them.'

'Let's hope it won't come to that.'

'You're sure this will work?' asked Kuro.

'Not a bit sure, but it's all we've got. If I fail, get yourself out of here and tell Kalaban.'

'Not before I kill that fat pig Gorgo,' replied the ninja coldly.

'I don't want to kill him,' said Trick. 'Just defeat him.'

'Trust me, Master Hope, it's the same thing. The only way you'll beat him *is* by killing him.'

'We'll see,' said Trick, limbering up. 'Now back up, mate. I don't want you to get hurt.' Kuro retreated, unsure what to make of the gallows humour.

'Remember – keep moving. Don't stand still. It's the only chance you have.'

Trick nodded before reaching inside his jacket. 'You're up, Sparky,' he whispered.

If Trick had been expecting some kind of wrestling MC to announce that the duel was under way, he was sorely disappointed. He first realized that the fight was on when a throwing knife hit the stone pillar beside his head. Masonry dust showered his face as Gorgo readied another blade.

'Start wriggling, worm!' he laughed.

Trick ran.

With his bamboo staff in hand, he hurdled the nearest waterway towards the darker recesses of the cavern, skidding behind a pillar. Shielded from the guildmaster's next attack, he looked down the length of his quarterstaff, spying light at the far end. It would be a squeeze, but it could work. Trick peered round the pillar in time to see Gorgo land on his side of the canal, his metal boots cracking the flags.

'There's nowhere to hide, worm, no hole you can wriggle into. Get some light over here, you lot!'

Upon his command, half a dozen torches were lobbed over the canal, skittering across the paved floor and illuminating the area. Alcoves and crypts suddenly flickered into view, leaving Trick with nowhere to run.

'Come out, come out, wherever you are.' Gorgo's giggle was sickly; the anticipation of the kill was getting the better of him.

Trick stepped out from behind the pillar, staff in hand. The torchlight shone off the guildmaster's plate-mail suit, the steel reflecting hellish red flames as he twirled two enormous knives in his hands.

'That's it?' said Gorgo. 'You think you can beat me with just a *stick*?'

'And a little help,' said Trick, raising the staff to his lips like an oversized pea-shooter. He aimed and blew hard, expelling a lungful of air into the blowpipe. The lightning bug – or Sparky, as Trick had named him – rocketed out of the other end, heading straight for the thief lord. Sparky had grown a bit since Trick had grabbed him in Grub Gulch, his diet of flies having kept him more than healthy. He struck Gorgo's breastplate dead centre, his hard carapace instantly connecting with the super-conductive metal. The lightshow that followed was breathtaking.

Trick was blinded momentarily as the electricity discharged into Gorgo lit him up like Piccadilly Circus. Sparks arced from him, leaping across the catacombs, finding the swords and daggers of his surrounding cronies. The thieves dropped their weapons, watching as smoke rolled out of the collar and cuffs of the guildmaster's steel suit. His daggers clattered to the floor as he dropped to his knees, the blue lightning dissipating.

Sparky hopped down from his chest, scuttling back across the flags towards Trick and narrowly missing being crushed by the toppling Gorgo as he crashed down like a felled redwood. His breastplate broke from its hinges and bounced clear, leaving the beaten guildmaster twitching spasmodically on the floor.

Trick's heart was racing. He couldn't quite believe his plan had worked. It had been a desperate roll of the dice, and somehow the gamble had paid off. He strolled forward on wobbly legs, trying to look confident while his insides were jelly. Walking past the still form of Gorgo, he stepped over the broken breastplate and came to a halt at the edge of the waterway. Across the canal he could see Kuro, surrounded by thieves. His face was hidden, but Trick was convinced the man was smiling.

'You have a choice,' said Trick. 'You don't *have* to work for a tyrant like Gorgo, and you *don't* have to remain under Boarhammer's boot. You can make a stand against injustice. Help your fellow men and women – free the slaves from the arena before they're murdered for fun. Are you with me?'

Some of the thieves turned to each other, the expressions on their faces shifting from fearful glares to hopeful glances. Trick could feel it: a growing sense of optimism. It wasn't shared by all, of course. Many of the guildmaster's most trusted men gathered together, forming a mean-looking huddle that simmered with ill intent. Trick held his breath, aware that the fight wasn't yet over.

'Trick!' yelled Kuro.

The boy turned just as Gorgo rose from the floor, shaking loose his broken armour and letting out a roar. Beneath the breastplate he wore a black jerkin, a white skull proudly emblazoned upon it: the unmistakable sign of a captain of the Skull Army. He held a dagger in each hand, raised, ready to strike the boy.

Then he halted, his eyes slowly dropping to his chest. A crossbow bolt was quivering in his exposed torso, quickly joined by five more. Gorgo fell for the second time that night. He landed on the flags with a crash, never to rise again.

Trick looked back at the throng of thieves, as did Kuro. The thieves lowered their crossbows, looks of contempt and dismay writ large upon their faces as they glared at the body of their master, their betrayer. Even those who had remained loyal to Gorgo had changed their tune, spitting curses at his corpse. The revelation of their master's true identity had a profoundly unifying effect upon them. The thieves stepped forward, shaking the ninja's hand and glancing Trick's way.

They stared at him with a mixture of awe and fascination. Trick's attention was drawn elsewhere though, towards the myriad tunnels and passageways that exited the chamber, disappearing into the cliffs that Sea Forge sat upon. Trick's sigh of relief nearly made him pass out.

Hope was winning.

# CHAPTER TWENTY-EIGHT

Trick was scared.

He'd suffered claustrophobia throughout his childhood, and had always feared being trapped in confined spaces – now he found himself stuck like a rat in a drainpipe. The tunnel was nearly vertical, and the rough-hewn walls provided foot- and handholds that helped him progress. However, the sewage and slurry that dripped and drizzled across the rocky surface made Trick's progress more perilous, as well as making him gag.

He fought back the urge to hurl, the only thing really stopping him being those who followed him up from below. The last thing they needed to contend with – alongside the poop walls and narrow tunnel – was Trick's breakfast showering down upon them. He felt a tug round his waist, as the rope suddenly yanked him from above, urging him to climb onwards, upwards.

As plans to infiltrate a villain's fortress arena went, this one had been straightforward. Kuro had been a key player in the plotting, the ninja apparently having had previous experience in this domain. Trick and his small army would crawl up through the network of sewers and storm drains that riddled the great cliffs of Sea Forge. Maps had been provided by the Thieves' Guild; there were few parts of the city that the band of rogues *didn't* know how to infiltrate. Eventually – if the climb didn't kill them – they would arrive in the ludus, the gladiators' training school. Erika had assured them that this would be empty on the day of a coliseum battle, with all the combatants gathered at the gates that ringed the arena.

From there it was a short sneak through one of the disused beast pens that were situated beneath the sand. Again, the Shield Maiden had helped here, knowing the layout of the tunnels beneath the arena better than anyone thanks to her days spent fighting for the amusement of Boarhammer. On occasion, and for added spice, the Skull Army would unleash creatures upon the gladiators, but that was a rarity. Of the eight pens that dotted the arena, Erika had guaranteed them that this one would be empty, as it had been turned into a storeroom.

Adjoining the pen they would find the slave cavern and, hopefully, their friends. Then it was simply a case of freeing the imprisoned warriors and launching a surprise assault on Boarhammer from within. They wouldn't even need to *enter* the arena; once they were in the marble halls and staircases of the coliseum, their victory should be a formality. Simple. Trick shuddered, still wondering how he'd found himself in this mess.

He glanced down as he climbed. His rope trailed below him, and the dim figure of a thief was visible four metres beneath him, illuminated by the hooded lantern that hung from Trick's belt. Its light flickered, the fuel just about exhausted. That was no surprise: they had been climbing for hours – throughout the morning – desperate to reach the Upper City before noon, for that was the allotted time for the contest to begin. According to Zuma, blood would be spilled in Boarhammer's arena once the sun was directly above Sea Forge.

Trick scrambled on, allowing his companions above to haul him upward. His thighs burned with the exertion, and his muscles ached with exhaustion. The lantern died its death now, the oil spent. High above he could hear a commotion, the sound of battle. The rope went slack suddenly, jarring Trick and knocking the lantern off the hook on his belt.

'Look out below!' he shouted as it bounced off the tunnel walls, shattering and showering hot glass over those who followed. There was no more progress on the rope. No more hauling from above. With a grunt and a groan, Trick dug his heels in and started to climb.

It was treacherous going. His hands were tattered, fingers useless, as all his adrenalin seemed spent. Trick used his fists, his knees and his elbows to clamber, putting every body part to work. Even his butt helped to anchor him as he wriggled and squirmed up the sewage-filled passageway.

Occasionally he felt those below slowing his progress as his rope went taut. His quarterstaff, shoved through a loop of leather on his belt, caught against the rocks. Ravenblade fared no better, the bird's-head pommel striking stone where it was stowed in a scabbard on his hip. Then above he saw a light, the mouth of the tunnel illuminated by sunlight. Trick hurried on, desperate to cover the remaining distance to the open air and the summit.

He emerged like a grub from the ground, coated in stinking slop and scores of scratches. Trick rolled on to his back and turned his head, coming face-to-face with the fellow who had been climbing ahead of him. The thief's eyes were wide, as was his stomach, his innards splashed across the floor. Trick squealed, shuffling clear as he looked around the chamber they'd arrived in.

The ludus was situated in a natural cavern beneath the arena, and the ground was littered with training apparatus and weapon racks. The embers of burnt-out fires smouldered in braziers around the room, the ludus having been abandoned, as Erika had said. Well, almost abandoned. The sewage chute they'd scrambled up had deposited Trick and his companions in the latrine, and there they had encountered a trio of Skull Army gladiators paying a last visit to the toilets before the glorious fight.

It had been a badly timed visit for both Boarhammer's warriors and the luckless thief who'd been killed in the subsequent melee. Two of the gladiators lay dead, dispatched by Zuma and Kuro. Trick wriggled clear of the tunnel mouth in time to see the third drop to his knees, with Erika's sword buried in his back. As he collapsed to the cold stone floor, she gave her weapon a twist, wrenching the blade free from her foe.

'Nothing's ever straightforward, is it?' said the Shield Maiden, flicking blood from the sword as she stalked across the ludus towards a great wooden door.

'Are you unharmed, Master Hope?' asked Kuro, reaching down to help Trick to his feet while more thieves began to emerge from the tunnel. Zuma and Kazumi assisted, dragging and lifting a steady stream of footpads and street ruffians out of the terrible sewer.

'Don't worry about me, mate,' said Trick, glancing down at the dead thief. 'What was his name?'

'Periwinkle,' said another brutish-looking thief who appeared beside them. 'And he was an idiot.'

'That's no way to speak of the dead,' said Kuro. 'That man gave his life for our cause.'

'You're noble all of a sudden, ninja. It don't suit you.'

'A man can change, Blocker.'

'Yeah? Well, that don't change the fact that Periwinkle was an idiot in life, and now he's an idiot in death.' He spat on the ground. 'I ain't gonna shed a tear for his loss. More booty for the rest of us to share out.'

Trick recognized Blocker now. He was one of the rogues who'd been closer to Gorgo than the others, probably a lieutenant or some such in the guildmaster's little army. Trick wasn't entirely convinced that Blocker shared his vision of a fairer, more caring Sea Forge for all.

'What happened to honour among thieves?' asked Trick. 'Periwinkle was a brother, wasn't he? A member of your noble guild. He deserves something more than a sneer and a spit, doesn't he?'

'He was a prat for going first with you and your warriors. If he'd had any smarts, he'd have hung back with me and the others, let you guys soak up any trouble in advance.'

Trick shook his head as the man strutted past. 'Wow. Do all thieves just look out for number one?'

Kuro considered Blocker carefully. 'They're not all like Blocker. He has more in common with his old master than you'd like to think.'

Now the gladiators were dead, Gorgo's former lieutenant was finding his voice and flexing his muscles, showing his fellow thieves that he was the closest thing the guild had to a new leader. He joined Erika by the wooden door, as the Viking held her ear to it.

'This the door through to the old pen, then?'

Erika looked him up and down and nodded.

'Stand aside then, girlie,' said Blocker. 'We'll take it from here.'

Erika stepped away from the door. 'After you, big man.'

Blocker pulled a crooked shortsword out of his belt as his closest comrades gathered round him. There were only a handful who looked up to the man.

'Beyond this door, we'll be into the coliseum proper. These guys want to take the fight to Boarhammer. Don't get in their way. You see anything of value, grab it. Anyone gives you trouble, you shiv 'em.' He gave his shortsword a twist in the air to drive home the point. 'We regroup back here in an hour's time. You got me?'

His cronies nodded, eyes lighting up greedily at the prospect of the booty they might get their hands on. Trick shook his head. They were better off without selfish swines like Blocker on their side. The big man grabbed the door handle.

'With me, lads!' he said, grinning as he threw open the door.

The grin remained on his face for only the briefest moment. An enormous scaly foot shot out from the chamber beyond, raking Blocker from head to toe. He teetered for a moment, face in ribbons, shocked and stunned, before the clawed limb seized him and yanked him into the pen. Only a fine spray of red mist remained where Gorgo's lieutenant had stood a second ago.

Erika twirled her sword and lifted her shield. 'Nothing's ever straightforward,' she repeated, and followed the dead thief into the room beyond.

# CHAPTER TWENTY-NINE

Trick hung back as Kazumi, Kuro and Zuma followed the Shield Maiden into the beast pen. *So much for it being unoccupied*, he mused anxiously. He clutched his quarterstaff in both hands, willing his courage to the fore as the sound of battle began to build. Blocker's companions looked less confident now, backing away from the door as other, braver thieves joined the heroes on the threshold. No sooner had the last man passed through the door than he was flung out once again, struck by a mighty blow, his broken body skidding along the floor and knocking more thieves off their feet.

'Right you are,' said Trick, unable to allow any more men to die in his name while he stood idly by. He raised the staff and dashed into the beast pen.

Daylight shone down from overhead through a ceiling grille, illuminating the chaos below. A great horned lizard, as tall as an elephant, filled the cavernous chamber, its six legs stamping the earth in fury as it lashed out at those who had invaded its holding pit. Zuma and Erika were on its back, hacking at it repeatedly with frenzied flurries, while Kuro hung beneath it, his katana buried in its throat.

Trick looked at the sword on his belt – Ravenblade – its black bird-headed handle poking out of the scabbard on his hip. The others had insisted he carry it into battle, even though he didn't intend to use it. No. He wasn't about to unsheathe it and jump into the melee. He was a school kid from London at the end of the day; he'd be as likely to kill himself or a friend as harm the monster. He brought his attention back to the giant lizard just in time to dive clear of its thrashing tail. Then Kazumi was on the ground, her footing lost as the beast moved in, its jaws wide open.

'This way, you big dumb lizard,' Trick shouted, the words out of his mouth before he'd even thought about it. He struck the staff on the ground, and the hollow pole sent sharp, echoing cracks bouncing off the rough-hewn walls of the pen. The monster followed him, turning away from Kazumi and advancing, while the heroes still clung to it, stabbing and slashing. Trick hit a wall as the lizard's jaws yawned open again, displaying rows of serrated teeth coated with scraps of torn and bloody flesh – the remains of Blocker, Trick figured.

The boy ducked as the beast's head struck the wall.

Trick dived to one side as the giant reptile pursued him. He'd bought his friend just enough time. Kazumi suddenly leapt out of the chamber's shadows, her naginata raised high before she thrust it down into one of the reptile's bulging eyes. Then Kuro was moving, ripping his katana out of the monster's throat as he rolled clear.

Bright green blood poured out after each attack, spraying the pen's floor as the behemoth collapsed on to its side. Zuma and Erika jumped clear as the lizard's long tail flickered and trembled like a rattlesnake in its death throes. Then the beast was still; the warriors were victorious.

The ninja stepped round the lizard's body, flicking green gloop off his katana as he offered to help Trick to his feet. The boy waved him away.

'I'm fine, Kuro. Are you though?'

The ninja was probably smiling beneath his black mask as he replied. 'Always good to stretch one's muscles ahead of a battle. Our reptilian friend has provided us with the perfect warm-up.' He slid his katana back into its scabbard on his back, before his eyes rested upon the black bird-headed sword on Trick's hip. 'Is she going to stay in there all day?'

'Don't you worry about Ravenblade,' said the boy, stepping over to the slain monster. 'I know exactly what I'm going to do with her. In the meantime I have my staff to protect me.'

He looked up at the roof of the cavern, where the huge grille separated them from the sand of the arena. Iron bars criss-crossed the entrance to the pit, hinged along one edge by an enormous mechanism. The Thieves' Guild maps and Erika's directions hadn't let them down. The sewer had brought them up through the cliffs and right into the heart of Boarhammer's playground. At the allotted time, the caged roof would descend, providing the resident horror its means of escape and access into the arena.

'I thought you said this pen would be unoccupied?' said Trick.

'That was news to me too,' said Erika. 'This chamber was a storeroom when I fought for Boarhammer. Makes me wonder . . . There were eight such pits in the arena, equidistant from each other; does each now contain its own horror?'

Trick gulped, doubt now nagging at him. He had imagined that their main threat would come from the gladiators who were paid to fight for Boarhammer, his champions recruited from the Skull Army. Those brutes were stone-cold killers, murderers who were paid to deal death in the arena. What's more, they loved their work. However, it appeared that there would be more than one monster joining them in the dust if this beast pen was anything to go by. The fight was becoming more daunting with each passing moment. The other warriors gathered round Trick, leaving the ever-growing horde of thieves to gather at their backs. Erika pointed to the rear of the chamber.

'That, my furious friends, is another problem.'

They all nodded. Even Trick saw it.

A portcullis blocked their exit from the room, running from the ceiling to the floor.

'Um, is that supposed to be there?' asked Trick.

Erika shook her head. 'Another recent modification. That gate is there to protect the beast keepers from the monsters in their charge,' she said, giving the lizard's corpse a boot. 'I've no idea how it's operated, and it bars our passage to the slave cavern. I'm sorry. I wasn't to know this would happen.'

Zuma muttered a curse under his breath.

'Was that directed at me?' hissed the Shield Maiden.

'And if it was? What then?' said the Jaguar Warrior defiantly.

'Can we not bicker,' sighed Kazumi, as Trick stepped up to the portcullis to inspect it.

How on earth were they supposed to reach Toki, Mungo and all the other prisoners now? They had intended to pass straight through here, enter the coliseum and cause havoc. Now they were trapped in a pit with a dead lizard, going nowhere fast. Trick looked at the iron gate, sizing it up. The gaps between the bars were too narrow for a brute like Zuma – or even Erika – to fit between. Not even Kuro would fit. There was only one among them who could get through and continue on to the slave cavern.

Trick thought for a moment. If he stayed behind in the pit until the roof grille descended, then it put the kibosh on all their plans. Trick had wanted to liberate the prisoners – including Toki and Mungo – who were shackled in the arena awaiting their death. Trick had wanted to speak to the crowd, to give them a chance to repent and disappear before the bloodshed and madness started. Trick had wanted to speak to Boarhammer, to give him a chance to surrender. He couldn't do any of that from the pit. Once the ramp had descended, all hell would break loose above and it would be every man and woman for themselves.

'I'll go on alone,' said Trick quietly, but his words were missed by the others who bickered behind him. '*I said* I'll go on to the slave cavern.'

'Quiet,' hissed Kuro to the others, silencing them as the mob of thieves watched nervously. 'You'll go through this gate alone? Are you sure, Master Hope?'

'I'm the only one who'll fit through the bars,' said the schoolboy. 'It has to be me. Besides, if I *am* the Black Moon Warrior, isn't it time I pulled my weight?'

He was joking of course, but the others took his words seriously. 'That's the spirit,' said Erika, clapping him on the back.

'Stay in the shadows, Master Hope,' said Kuro.

'Remember all I've told you. Step lightly, strike swiftly – the darkness is your friend.'

'Right you are,' said Trick, rolling his eyes.

'When the roof descends,' said Zuma, 'we shall be by your side!'

'I know. Until then I'm on my own,' added the boy.

'We'll be right behind you, Trick,' said Kazumi.

'Yeah, behind this portcullis,' he said, handing his gear to Zuma before slowly squeezing between the bars. His ribs felt like they might split as he turned his head sideways, his ears and skull scraping against the rusted iron. He could hear the crowd above, their cheers and chants. Trick could feel his insides gnawing away with anxiety at the task that lay ahead. Perhaps if this *were* all a dream, and he climbed into the arena, a well-placed blow from an enemy's axe might be just the thing to wake him up. A violent jolt to stir him from this mother-of-all-nightmares. He fell through to the other side of the portcullis and turned back to his comrades.

Or perhaps it might just kill him.

# CHAPTER THIRTY

The guards stood at the gate to the slave cavern, rattling their swords against the lowered portcullis. While one held a guttering torch in his hand – the flame illuminating his pockmarked face – his companion couldn't resist taunting their prisoners.

'Don't worry, boys and girls,' said the Skull Army veteran. 'Your moment in the sun is just round the corner. We're taking you up top any moment. If I were you, I'd say my goodbyes now.'

His friend laughed, giving him a dig in the back, as the pair of them walked away, returning to their guard room. Only when they had gone did Trick separate himself from the shadows. He peeled away from the darkness, having been hidden mere metres away from the pair of bullies.

He danced lightly down the corridor, his sure-footed

parkour skills carrying him smoothly and silently towards the portcullis. It was just like the one in the beast pen. Perhaps it was operated by a lever in the guard room? He glanced towards the light that flickered round the corner of the corridor. No, he wasn't about to pursue that theory. Unbuckling his belt, he passed it through the bars, followed by his staff. Beyond, through the rails, he could see pale eyes watching him. Frightened eyes.

With no small degree of pain and discomfort, Trick forced himself between the bars, landing in an ungainly heap within the slave pen. The prisoners nearest to him backed away, alarmed by the arrival of a stranger in their midst. Who was this, who would willingly climb through the portcullis to join them? Men and women backed away, children hiding behind their parents as Trick picked up his gear and went deeper into the cavern.

Most of the prisoners were recognizably civilians, like those who had been rounded up in Warriors Landing. Their ragged clothes were torn and stained with blood, their faces dark with grime and dirt. As Trick advanced and the captives retreated, he heard their manacles jangling, a grim chorus of grating metal, as their shackled feet carried them clear of him. Then he was through the terrified poor folk, and approaching another row of bars. Beyond this barrier he could see the imprisoned warriors.

They stood in a cluster, a dozen of them, shoulder to

shoulder, their backs turned as they plotted a plan of action. Their time in the arena was at hand. Chained they may be, but none of them intended going down without a fight. Trick heard their voices, some in agreement, some arguing, as they decided how they should fight. The debate was fierce, their pitch rising, some even shoving one another.

'Not more bickering warriors,' muttered Trick, as one of them turned to face him.

Then another spun round, followed by a further two. Within seconds, the whole gang of manacled fighters was facing the boy from London and staring him down. Suddenly they were parted and the closest two pushed to one side as a familiar figure came staggering out of the huddle. Trick would have recognized the youth's bright red hair anywhere. The Norseman rushed over to Trick and embraced him through the bars, only disengaging to bump fists.

'Toki, my friend. You cannot imagine how good it is to see you!'

'Friend, Trick? You're my brother! I knew you would come!'

'Yeah. Fancy seeing you here, mate,' said Trick, his laughter verging on delirious as he looked about him. The murmur in the crowd of warriors was building now as more and more of them drew closer.

'Where's Mungo?'

The Viking clapped Trick's shoulder and pointed

beyond his cell, across the cavern towards another crowd of captives. The blue-woad warrior stood among them, but showed no sign of recognition when the two of them waved at him.

'Our painted friend isn't all there,' said Toki, tapping his temple. 'I fear he is witless. What's your plan?'

'I mean to speak with the fat clown in the tower.'

'Speak to Boarhammer? That's your plan?'

'Oh, there's a little more to it than that,' said Trick, smiling.

He unbuckled his weapon belt and handed it through the bars to the Viking. Toki snapped the gear on and seized the handle of the sword. Out it came from its scabbard, smooth and silent.

'Ravenblade?' gasped the Norseman.

'We found her, Toki! We found Boneshaker's sword. And I want you to use it in my place, mate.' For a moment he thought the red-haired Viking might cry. Trick patted his shoulder as his friend gripped the sword. 'I won't let you down, brother.'

'See that you don't,' said Trick with a wink. 'Listen, you need to free as many people as you can, Toki, now, before the fighting starts. They're gonna send you up there chained together. Use the sword and start breaking those manacles. That'll be a surprise Boarhammer isn't expecting, nor his gladiators for that matter.'

'I like your thinking, Trick. By Odin's chin, we will die a glorious death!'

'No, Toki!' said Trick, annoyance clear in his voice. His hand went through the bars and grabbed his friend by the jerkin. 'Nobody's going out with a glorious death today. No blaze of glory or slow-motion shoot-out. I want you – I want *everyone* here – to get out of this mess alive. Do you hear me?'

Toki nodded, suitably admonished. 'I do, Trick. I do. It's just . . . Boarhammer must answer for his crimes.'

'And he will. Me, Erika, Kuro and the others have that covered.'

'Erika?' said the Viking, his dirty face lighting up. 'You have found my kinswoman, the Shield Maiden.'

'I have,' grinned Trick. 'Bit of a head-the-ball, isn't she?' Toki's blank reaction prompted Trick to elaborate. 'She seems to have a lot of anger issues.'

That made Toki smile. 'If she's anything like the women from my village, she's a strong, powerful warrior.'

'She is that, and then some,' sighed Trick. He looked around, seeing that everyone had huddled round them now, warriors and peasants alike.

'You all heard what I said?' he hissed. They nodded. 'We'll need anyone who can swing a staff to be ready. And those of you who can't – women, children, old folk – as soon as things kick off, get out of there and back down here. The Thieves' Guild will be causing chaos throughout the coliseum if all goes according to plan.'

They all nodded and muttered enthusiastically, acknowledging the plan. *Plan*, mused Trick. That was a stretch as a description.

'Toki, once the guards come, you need to hide that sword under your cloak. Don't let them see it. I don't think they want any warriors heading out there with enchanted legendary weapons, mate.'

'I hear you, Trick,' said the Viking. 'You'd better go now. They'll be back shortly.'

'I'm going nowhere,' said Trick, stepping among the peasants and trying his best to blend in.

'What are you saying?'

'I'm coming with you guys. I'm joining you in the arena.'

# CHAPTER THIRTY-ONE

The mood inside Boarhammer's arena had intensified, anticipation of the forthcoming bloodshed whipping the crowd into a frenzy. There was a party atmosphere on the terraces, as the privileged of Sea Forge united in song and celebration. The noise was overwhelming: the spectators sang bawdy, tasteless tunes and chanted the names of their favourites. It reminded Trick of the one occasion he'd been to the football, a windswept afternoon spent at the Emirates Stadium with his dad. That had been his single flirtation with soccer.

The sport wasn't for Trick: far too tribal and intimidating. Not like Boarhammer's arena, of course. Oh no, there was nothing at all scary about the place he now found himself in. The outlandishly dressed teenage boy stepped through the prisoners and made his way towards the warlord's viewing tower. Skinny jeans and a school blazer provided the most eye-catching and unlikely gladiatorial armour.

Trick didn't run. There seemed little point. He was here to attract Boarhammer's attention after all. And, after the portcullis complication, it had to be him who did this. Just Trick's luck. There were perhaps a hundred people in the arena, gathered together in huddles. Some among them were warriors, snatched from the streets of Sea Forge by the Skull Army. Most of them were no doubt from the Broken Shield Inn, Trick realized. They'd been handed blunt, broken, rusty weapons with which to defend themselves, and clubs and staffs as well.

Many of the captives he'd climbed into the arena with were here simply as cannon fodder. All were chained together by manacles, restricting their movement and chances of survival. Or so Boarhammer and the Skull Army thought.

He took in the captive warriors and peasants as he walked among them. The slaves held battered old swords and shields fearfully. His heart skipped a beat when he spied the child from Warriors Landing. *What kind of monster would throw an infant into the arena?* Trick wondered. The girl was clutching her father's thigh, her eyes fixed on Trick just as they had been the day she was abducted from her village. He wondered if she'd yet shed a tear. Perhaps a quick death would be the most she could pray for after the horrors she'd endured. Her eyes followed him as he passed by.

The warriors were intrigued to see this strange boy without shackles and chains. Of course, those who had been in Toki's cell were anticipating what was to come. They winked and nodded at him as he continued on his way. These were no favourites of Boarhammer; they were from Trick's home, if not time. He spied a dark-skinned Aborigine, a knight in armour and a swashbuckling pirate with a colourful bandana; they were many, transported to this world of warriors by magic. Trick caught their eyes, hoping he could count on them when the moment came. They gave little away.

Then there were Boarhammer's gladiators. These were professional fighters who traded in death; this day promised to be glorious and bloody for them. Only those gladiators loyal to Boarhammer were given the freedom of the sand, and they stalked over it, gladly receiving the applause of the bloodthirsty crowd. They were soldiers from his elite troops, the Blackguard, happy to take up arms against hamstrung warriors and shackled slaves. These were the crowd's champions, their glorious killers. They *wanted* to be there.

Trick looked up at the towering wooden viewing platform that overlooked the battleground. A huge golden gong hung shining like the sun from the back of the balcony, dominating the viewing deck. Boarhammer's guests of honour were taking their seats, protected from the noon sun's rays by a great red velvet canopy.

Trick spied both men and women up there, laughing, drinking and dining as they took up positions on the balcony. Each was dressed in finery – the men in flowing robes, the women adorned with gaudy gems and jewels. These were Boarhammer's cronies, the lickspittles who helped him run Sea Forge and the surrounding region: merchants, slavers and sea captains. And there, at the centre of the crowd of fawning opportunists, was the man himself.

Boarhammer was as broad as he was tall, his jutting jaw constantly flapping as he entertained his guests, laughing at his own jokes – the king of all he surveyed. A huge mace swung from his hip, his bone-breaking weapon of choice. Its golden head was studded with spikes, and looked profoundly brutal. The warlord had built his reputation with that terrible hammer, his berserk rages having claimed a long list of victims across the length and breadth of the Wildlands, all in the name of Boneshaker. These days, however, the mace was just for show. His old armour and infamous boar's-head helm gathered dust in his palace armoury; the warlord had let himself go in dramatic fashion. His belly juddered, his jowls wobbled, wine was spilled and lumps of chewed meat were spat from his mouth. He was truly grotesque.

The crowd had spotted Trick now, and a murmur rippled through them as they shouted, screamed and pointed. One of Boarhammer's gladiators rushed to intercept him, dashing between the chained warriors and peasants as he came upon the teenager unawares. The man hadn't reckoned on one of the shackled warriors though. Hands reached out, grabbing him by the skull and with a swift crack his neck was broken. Trick heard the sickening sound and glanced back. Toki nodded grimly, his hand returning to the jet-black sword beneath his cloak.

'Remember, be ready for anything,' Trick said to his friend, before striding closer to Boarhammer's wooden tower.

He had their attention now, as the warlord's guests crowded along the balcony's railing.

'A filthy urchin!' shouted one man.

'A slave has escaped!' screamed a woman.

'Kill it, quickly!' ordered a white-robed boy, pointing out the intruder to the Blackguard gladiators. He was standing beside Boarhammer, and the warlord's hand was placed gently and lovingly upon his mop of bright blond hair. Was this the favourite nephew Kalaban had warned him about? He was probably a year younger than Trick, but already showed signs of becoming a full-fledged monster. Four of Boarhammer's elite soldiers weaved their way through the imprisoned combatants now, keen to reach their quarry. Trick wasted no more time.

'Hear me, people of Sea Forge,' shouted Trick, and the amphitheatre fell suddenly quiet.

The blond-haired boy rushed to the balcony's railing and shoved his master's guests aside. 'Silence him!' yelled the child, his face flushed red with rage.

'Let him speak!'

They all turned at the sound of the voice, rich as syrup, dripping with cocksure confidence. The Lord of Sea Forge rose from his throne on the balcony.

'But he has their ears, Uncle,' said the boy, pointing at Trick below. Three of Boarhammer's gladiators had stepped before Trick now, holding their position as they awaited orders from above. 'He could poison them with his lies.'

'Are you truly afraid of what one boy might say, young Hugo? Do you have that little faith in our subjects? Our people?'

'Heavens, no,' said the fair-haired boy sheepishly, returning to his position beside the throne.

Boarhammer leaned on the balcony, his huge golden mace clattering noisily against the railing. His smile was hideous, his chin and jowls slick with grease, fat and food remnants. 'You think you can sway them to your side? Go on then. Try it. Choose your words wisely, child. They're your last.'

Boarhammer's words echoed, distant and hollow. Trick was busy looking at the trio of gladiators who stood before him. He slowly retreated, returning to the pit he'd emerged from. The gladiators followed. All the while he spoke loudly and clearly to the bloodthirsty audience.

'Pigmallet seems to think I'm here to convince you to join forces with me – ditch him and hook up with my gang. Well, that's not what I'm here to do.' The crowd hadn't expected that, and looked at one another with a mixture of bemusement and bafflement.

'I'm telling you to go. Leave now. Don't come back. This arena's closed for business. As for Pigmallet, he ain't your master any more. The *real* people of Sea Forge are taking their city back, all those poor sods you keep down by the docks: fish-gutters, clam-diggers, poop-shovellers and street-sweepers. Your time's over, you shower of sickos. You can just disappear. Leave the arena. Leave the city. Never come back. You ain't welcome here, see?'

There was silence on the arena terraces for the briefest time. Could the strange, gangly boy *really* be saying this? Were the upper classes of Sea Forge really witnessing this bizarre speech? As they realized it was some ridiculous joke, some jape that Boarhammer had planned as part of the spectacle, they burst out laughing. Some of them cheered. Most of them simply spat obscenities at Trick.

None of them left the arena.

'Was that what you hoped for?' asked a triumphant Boarhammer on his balcony.

'No. But it's what I expected.'

Before Trick could say another word, there was a resounding clang of metal that made his teeth hum. The gong reverberated, Boarhammer's weapon having struck it dead centre. Right on cue, there was a grinding of metal as levers, winches and other mechanisms set to work beneath the arena. The metal grilles dropped on their hinges, transforming from bars into ramps. There were cheers from the crowd, screams from the slaves and war cries from the warriors as Boarhammer's pets clambered out of their pits.

'Please let this work,' whispered Trick, as chaos reigned.

# CHAPTER THIRTY-TWO

As the trapdoors clanged open, they sent great plumes of sand billowing across the arena. Gladiators, warriors and slaves alike covered their faces against the choking sand clouds as they slowly subsided. Trick could hear the roar of the crowd, wild with feverish anticipation of the horror that was to come. He blinked as the air slowly cleared.

Monsters of all shapes and sizes emerged from the pits. They crept and crawled, slithered and swooped, a host of otherworldly beasts. A feather-maned mountain lion was first from its pit, hackles raised and black quills rippling. Its roar heralded the arrival of the rest. An enormous white-furred ape followed, fists beating its chest as it let loose a roar, straight out of an old monster movie.

A centipede the length of a double-decker bus

scuttled up another ramp, weaving straight for a gaggle of slaves. With a beating of leathery wings, four bat-like creatures emerged from their pen, canine heads snarling. They were all chained to a single great boulder which they dragged across the sand as they snapped at each other, seeking a likely meal.

Trick blinked away the sand as the three armour-clad men closed on him. He peered over his shoulder at the pit he had squeezed out of; the ramp grille was lowered, and nothing was emerging. It was the merest snapshot of a glance before his eyes were back upon the trio. They wore chain vests and gladiatorial helmets and – judging by their chuckles – they were grinning inside them. Would they ever have an easier kill than this kid? Trick's chest went tight as if crushed within a giant's fist. He grimaced, fearing his organs might fail before the thugs even reached him. *Thirteen years old*, he mused. *No age for a heart attack.* The gladiators raised their weapons in unison, readying to strike him.

The wind whipped around Trick's ears as figures leapt past him, bounding from the pit at his back. The three fighters stopped short, each faltering where he stood. They were no longer alone. A warrior crouched beside each of them. Zuma, Kuro and Kazumi had dealt their counterparts killing blows, but the gladiators didn't yet know it. It only dawned upon them as bright red wounds opened across their broken armour and they fell into the sand, wheezing and gurgling. Zuma shook his macuahuitl over his head, Kuro flicked blood from his katana and Kazumi twirled her naginata.

Then Trick's companions were moving, dispersing into the assembled prisoners to break their bonds. They weren't alone. The warriors who had already been freed by Trick and Toki provided cover, engaging the Blackguard gladiators and keeping them occupied. Chains were struck, links were broken and slaves and warriors were set free.

'You did well, Trick Hope,' said Erika, arriving beside him as a mob of thieves followed her from the pit. Having clambered up the enormous butchered corpse of the monstrous lizard, they scrambled on to the sand, seeking out foes. Women and children dashed the other way, urged towards the tunnels and safer places by a handful of veteran career criminals. The younger thieves were armed with their favourite light arms: clubs and daggers, crossbows and slings.

'You think?' asked Trick. 'Reckon I just got Boar-hammer mad!'

'That's a good thing. His anger makes him reckless and that will be his downfall. Kuro and Kazumi will bring him down. We all have our part to play in the fight. Remember, yours is to stay close to me. Leave the fighting to us warriors. You *don't* leave my side.'

As if to emphasize this point she raised her shield before them, catching an arrow in the wood with a resounding *thunk*. Trick nodded.

'I'm cool with that!'

He didn't need telling twice. Trick was more than happy that the Shield Maiden was his protector. Climbing into the arena had taken all his remaining nerve after his duel with Gorgo. He was a spent force now, his legs trembling as the battle raged around them.

'No time like the present,' said Erika, reaching over her shoulder to where a bundle of spears was holstered. Trick fixed his gaze upon the supposedly impregnable tower, only accessible via the corridors and avenues that circuited the amphitheatre. Trick prayed that the Shield Maiden had as good an aim as he believed. He'd seen her skill with a spear on the docks when she'd pinned Kuro to the floor. As if in answer, her first spear hit the bottom of the tower, reverberating where it buried itself in the timber.

The plan was bold. By peppering the warlord's tower with her spears, Erika would provide Kuro and Kazumi with a route to Boarhammer's balcony. The ninja and samurai would then scale the fortified tower and dispatch the Lord of Sea Forge. Two more spears found their mark, wobbling where they struck the timber of the tower. Trick's thoughts returned to Toki as he searched the arena for his friend once more.

With the Thieves' Guild joining the fray, confusion reigned, and the Skull Army rushed in from the main gates to the aid of their gladiator brethren. Soon thieves and slaves were locked in mortal duels with

Boarhammer's forces. All the while, monsters kicked and clawed, bit and bashed, attacking the combatants indiscriminately.

Trick even spied the drunken gladiator who had brawled with Mungo and Zuma in the Broken Shield Inn – Crixus, he'd called himself. He was there in the middle of the melee, trident in hand, seeking out his foes. It was hard to tell whose side he was on, so chaotic was the battle. Of course, Trick's warrior companions were causing the most damage. Trying to keep track of them made his head spin.

Kuro and Kazumi fought back to back, katana and naginata slashing about them and finding man and monster as they made their way ever closer to Boarhammer's tower and their makeshift steps. The two made a great team, their movements almost balletic as they cut a swathe through their foes in the sand.

Zuma was a blur, darting between the armoured men, his macuahuitl splitting steel and breaking bones. The Jaguar Warrior's face was a mask of grim delight. With a shiver, Trick realized the Aztec *enjoyed* this, revelled in the kill. He wasn't alone, either. Mungo was now free from his bonds, shouting and screaming as he straddled the giant centipede. He rode it across the sand, grasping its antennae as he steered it over the Skull Army. They shrieked as they were crushed beneath its hundred clawed feet, while the blue-woad warrior whooped with berserk, bloody glee.

Then Trick saw Toki.

The young Viking stood beneath the four dog-headed bat creatures that were chained to the boulder. With a swipe of Ravenblade, he hacked at the links of one of the chains, shards of twisted iron flying. The monster beat its wings, chancing a bite at the red-haired youth. He smacked it away with the flat of the blade, sending it flapping clear. Catching the broken length of chain in his free hand, Toki quickly bound it round his arm and ran after the creature, his feet kicking up sand.

'Toki!' screamed Trick, almost distracting Erika from her task.

If the young Viking heard Trick, he didn't show it, and the Norseman allowed the bat monster to take flight. It tried to escape the arena, only for Toki to poke and prod it with the sword, guiding it in another, far more dangerous direction.

'Oh God,' whispered Trick.

'What?' asked Erika, firing another spear across the arena and finding her target.

'He's going for Boarhammer,' said the boy. 'Alone!'

Dumb instinct kicked in suddenly and unexpectedly. Trick dashed headlong across the bloodstained sand towards the warlord's tower.

'Come back!' the Shield Maiden shouted. 'Trick!'

'He needs my help. Keep those spears coming!' the boy called back, ducking beneath the lunging attacks of gladiators, guards and gargantuan monsters. He looked up as he ran. Toki was directly overhead, gliding towards the balcony, the bat-beast snarling as he steered it towards the tower's top. Trick didn't have a clue what he was doing. This was rash to the point of suicidal, but he couldn't allow his friend to fight Boarhammer and his cronies alone.

Trick channelled all his concentration into his frantic dash, pushing the fear from his mind and ignoring his aching limbs. He skidded under a scything sword swipe like a world-class limbo dancer before hurdling the low chop of a pole-arm. He swung out his quarterstaff, cracking a gladiator across the wrist and snapping the bones, before bringing it round before him. Then he was at the foot of the tower, driving the end of the staff into the sand. It dug in, the staff bending as Trick used it like a vaulting pole. It propelled him high towards the first spear, three metres off the ground, then clattered to the ground behind him.

The Shield Maiden was a wizard with weapons, but agility was Trick Hope's forte. The sure-footed nimbleness that had made the rooftops of London his playground now came to his aid. He caught the spear shaft and swung, hauling himself on to it with the agility of a spider monkey. The next spear was already above him, followed by a third. He glanced quickly towards Erika and saw the Viking concentrating on hitting her mark, before he leapt for spear number two. Then he was moving, finding rhythm, the momentum carrying him higher like a gymnast on the bars.

Trick was halfway up the tower when he heard a hideous howl from the bat creature above. Peppered with arrows and crossbow bolts, the monster began to tumble from the air, some way short of the balcony. Toki was moving, scrambling up its tumbling body and making a leap for the tower top.

Trick caught sight of his friend disappearing on to Boarhammer's viewing deck, to a chorus of screams, cheers and jeers. The winged monstrosity was plummeting now, snapping the two uppermost spears from the tower wall, bouncing off the supporting beams. Trick hugged the timber panels as it tumbled by, narrowly missing him.

Suddenly he was stuck, twelve metres up the tower, but four metres below the balcony. He could hear the fighting up there, and heard Toki's roar as he engaged the enemy. Trick glanced desperately back at the arena.

No sign of Zuma; the Jaguar Warrior was lost in the melee. Kuro and Kazumi remained surrounded by the enemy, bloodied but unbeaten, unable to reach him. Mungo had switched beasts, ditching the slaughtered centipede for a great purple toad. Its hide was peppered with arrows, as was the blue-woad warrior, but he rode it with deft skill as they trampled the enemy in bone-crunching bounds.

The battle still raged, but Erika stood motionless in

the eye of the maelstrom. Her spears were all gone and only her shield remained. She immediately understood Trick's desperate look and nodded.

Erika took a deep breath and aimed. The shield spun through the air like a discus, rising higher as it neared the tower. Trick gasped as it hit the wood above his head, splitting it as the metal edge buried itself deep in the dark timber. He crouched and leapt, snatching at the shield's rim. He grabbed hold, struggling and scrambling to clamber on to its battered surface. He looked up. The distance to the balcony had been halved. He jumped off the shield and the makeshift ledge gave him greater power, like a diver's springboard.

Trick caught the railing just as one of Boarhammer's soldiers peered over the edge. The boy grabbed the chinstrap of his helmet and yanked him down, smashing the guard's face into the railing. He went limp. Muscles burning, Trick crawled up and over the man's unconscious body and arrived on the warlord's balcony.

The scene was freeze-framed for Trick. The horrible drawn-out moment was captured as time seemed to slow. Toki crouched low as eight of the warlord's best soldiers encircled him, their master hovering behind them. Wounds criss-crossed Toki's body, inflicted by the gaggle of brutes. They coaxed an attack from him, drawing him on to the offensive. It worked. As the Norseman lashed out with Ravenblade, tearing a bloody gash through the nearest two Skull Army soldiers,

Boarhammer leapt in. His spiked mace descended, striking Toki with such ferocity that it broke the Viking's helmet in two.

Toki went down in a heap, red hair darkening as blood spread from the fresh wound. Boarhammer shoved his men aside and stood over him triumphantly, his mace raised once more. Trick's heart stopped beating, frozen in his chest as he foresaw his friend's fate. He saw Ravenblade on the floor, dropped when Toki had been felled. He was beaten, perhaps already dead. If he wasn't, the killing blow was about to fall. The mace was dropping when Trick leapt, snatching up the black sword as he threw himself between friend and foe.

# CHAPTER THIRTY-THREE

Ravenblade flew straight and true in Trick's outstretched hand, intercepting the terrible golden mace. He caught the weapon's head with the flat of the black stone sword, expecting the reverberations to explode through his arm – or at the very least that Ravenblade would shatter.

Instead there was a shock of blue lightning as sparks erupted up and down her length, runes flashing into life along the obsidian shaft as Boarhammer's spiked mace was deflected. The warlord's cry of horror was a high-pitched shriek of pain and outrage, as he tumbled into his men. Trick landed upon Toki's body in an ungainly tangle of limbs as he raised the sword again and flashed her at his enemies. The Skull Army soldiers hesitated.

'Speak to me, Toki,' hissed Trick, his eyes never leaving the assembled soldiers.

The men advanced now, their initial shock at the boy's dramatic arrival subsiding. Trick knew what they were thinking, could see it in their eyes as they snarled and grimaced. He may have stopped their boss's attack, but he was just a kid, right?

'You impress me, boy,' said Boarhammer, his voice a gurgle that choked back his pain. 'I can find a place for you in my master's ranks. You have pluck. Nerve.'

Trick was lost for a response, before falling back on the timeless insult of spitting and sneering. Boarhammer returned the sneer.

'Shame if you have to die today, boy, but if your heart is set upon it . . .'

Trick ignored the warlord, instead nudging his friend where he lay.

'Tell me you're alive, Toki!'

There was a spluttering cough from the floor at last. 'You think I die that easily?'

A fist rose into the air, wavering before Trick. He gave it a quick bump with his free knuckles before turning to Boarhammer.

'It's over, Pigmallet. Call off your dogs or they die a heartbeat before you.'

'You think you scare me? A lone boy before my Blackguard?'

The sunlight flickered on the assembled combatants as dark shapes flitted above them and shadows flashed over the group. Two figures landed on either side of

Trick, one in a battle-ravaged kimono, the other clad in black.

'Who said he was alone?' hissed Kuro, as Kazumi twirled her naginata.

Trick's grin was fierce; the odds had suddenly improved. He picked up a piece of Toki's broken helmet, feeling the metal's jagged edge rough against his palm.

'Two more craven cretins to be slaughtered,' laughed Boarhammer. 'It's been far too long since I killed a man, or woman for that matter. I shall enjo–'

His boast was cut short as the shard of broken helmet struck him between the eyes, splitting the bridge of his nose.

'You talk too much, Pigmallet,' said Trick, as Kuro and Kazumi sprang forward.

Boarhammer might have been stunned, but his men were ready. They met katana and naginata with raised weapons, the deafening clash making Trick's skull ring and teeth hum. The two warriors each had three Blackguards to contend with, trading blades and blows, swords and slashes. All the while the ninja and samurai kept the enemy away from the boy and their fallen comrade, fending off the attacks. Trick dragged Toki clear towards the balcony's edge, away from the heart of the battle.

'It's OK, Toki,' he said, patting his friend's shoulder where he was slumped. 'Stay with me, mate. Just stay with me.'

Trick looked up just as the battle took a bizarre turn for the worse. Through the brawling warriors and soldiers, he caught sight of Boarhammer raising his giant golden mace. Trick didn't have time to wonder what the veteran warlord was doing. Boarhammer threw his head back, squealing like a stuck pig, a stream of unintelligible words erupting from his frothing lips. With horror, Trick realized that the berserker of old had returned.

Then the golden mace came crashing down, the enraged Lord of Sea Forge driving it into the wooden planks as if he were delivering the coup de grâce upon his most hated foe. The tower shook, timbers bowing and breaking as a great shockwave seized it. The fighters fell into one another, losing both footing and composure in that moment of madness.

A gulf opened up across the balcony as it rocked and swayed, torn apart by the mighty blow. Three of Boarhammer's men tumbled into it, screaming and wailing as they fell into its depths, torn apart upon spears of splintered wood below.

Toki suddenly slid towards the yawning chasm. Trick moved fast, hooking his leg through the balcony railing and reaching for his friend. He grabbed Toki's shoulder with his left hand, briefly halting his progress. Trick felt his fingers straining, knuckles popping, as the Viking slipped from his grasp. His locked leg gave, sending the pair of them a metre closer to the drop before his foot found the railing again.

'Let me go, Trick,' wheezed Toki. 'Better I fall than both of us.'

'I won't let you die,' shouted Trick, raising Raven-blade in his right hand.

The sword came down as he released Toki's shoulder, cutting into the collar of the Viking's cloak and sinking into the timbers of the sundered tower. The black blade remained in place, as the ragged, green cloth tore a little more while Toki slowed. He dangled over the edge, saved for now, his cloak held fast. Trick frantically grabbed the balcony railing, hauling himself upright as he looked over the arena.

The fighting had spread below, thieves and slaves side by side on the sand and terraces. Fires burned, torches having been put to Boarhammer's arena as the poor and unfortunate fought back. Sea Forge's wealthiest citizens screamed as they fled, aghast that the unsavoury spectacle now threatened them. The tower shuddered and the deck shifted beneath Trick, as if he were on a sinking ship. It was coming down, without a doubt, and when it did they would all go with it.

Across the swaying, shuddering balcony he caught sight of Kuro, wrestling with a foe. His katana was gone from his hand, and the Blackguard held a knife to the ninja's throat. The two teetered momentarily, before a shockwave shook the tower and they toppled over the side, still locked in their deadly embrace.

That left just Kazumi. She faced the two remaining

soldiers of Boarhammer's retinue, and her naginata snagged one and tossed his bleeding body aside.

A fat hand suddenly slapped Trick hard across the face. He fell to his knees, head spinning and vision blurring. Trick brought his gaze back to Boarhammer, and saw the Lord of Sea Forge standing over him.

'You're a plucky sprat, I'll give you that. Seems a shame to kill you.'

'Kill him, Uncle!' came a reed-thin voice from the rear of the tower, where the blond-haired child's face poked out from behind the velvet curtains.

Boarhammer waved a heavy, jewelled hand to silence his nephew. 'Quiet, Hugo. All in good time.'

Behind the warlord, Trick spied Kazumi dispatching the last of the combatants. She spun, eyes fixed on Boarhammer. The warlord berserker caught the look on Trick's face and began to turn.

'The bigger they come,' said Trick hastily, holding Boarhammer's attention, 'the harder they fall. That's what they say, right?'

It bought the samurai the time she needed. She leapt, weapon high, over the yawning chasm towards Boarhammer's back. Trick's heart soared as she pounced, only to break in his chest a split second later. A long-shafted arrow shot up from the arena, ripping through her so she spun in mid-air. Her naginata flew from her hands, and then she too was falling, swallowed by the widening gap in the broken timbers, until she was lost from sight. All that was left was the arrow, quivering in the wall at the balcony's back, black feathers stained red. Boarhammer caught the naginata without looking, an outstretched hand reaching behind his back.

'My compliments to the archer,' he shouted, his voice gurgling within his monstrous, heaving chest. He held the naginata forward, the blade wobbling beneath Trick's chin. The steel tip lifted the black moon pendant where it rested against the sweating hollow of the boy's throat. 'What an intriguing trinket . . . What is that? A crescent moon? Where did you get such a thing?'

Trick couldn't speak. He was paralysed with fear.

'He's the Black Moon Warrior, you fat tub of guts,' said Toki, wheezing where he hung over the chasm. 'If you haven't already heard of him, you will do. Your time's over, Boarhammer. My friend will bring your master to his knees.'

'The "Black Moon Warrior", eh? I'm sure Boneshaker is quaking in his boots. My master will be so pleased to receive your head.' The naginata cut the cord and with a deft flick Boarhammer tossed the pendant in the air. He caught it in a pudgy hand. 'Pick up your sword, boy. Defend yourself.'

Trick remained on his knees, still shocked by what had happened to Kazumi. She had been there one second, gone the next. Death was that fast?

'Your sword, boy,' repeated Boarhammer, the hideous voice stirring Trick from his shattered thoughts. He looked at Ravenblade, buried in the floor, the only thing preventing Toki from sharing Kazumi's fate. Smoke was billowing from the chasm now – the base of the tower had clearly been put to the torch.

'I can't,' said Trick. 'My friend. The sword.'

'It's easy,' said Boarhammer, inspecting Kazumi's naginata as the battle raged around them and the fires continued to spread. 'Take the blade.'

'If I do, my friend will die.'

'If you don't, you will die.'

'I won't . . . I can't do it.'

'I'll make it easy for you, then.'

The naginata whipped out, striking Ravenblade and tearing her free from where she was buried in the floorboards. The sword landed in Trick's lap as Toki disappeared over the edge, swallowed by the smoking ravine.

'*No!*' screamed Trick, pouncing on Boarhammer with such speed that the warlord was thrown. Perhaps he'd expected the boy to pick up the sword and figured that would be the attack he'd need to parry. As it was, he raised the naginata too late, and the weapon was ineffective, Trick having closed the distance in a blink of an eye. His attack was like nothing Boarhammer had ever faced: a flurry of wild, seemingly uncoordinated strikes. They were anything but for Trick, though. He was transported back to middle school in that instant, facing Big Ben Barker, the bully who had tormented him throughout his childhood.

Trick was the berserker.

His shoulder struck Boarhammer in the guts, making him double up. Trick's heel caught him in the shin, sending him stumbling. His hands clawed at the man's face, leaving red slashes in their wake. Elbows jabbed and knees came up as Trick frenziedly attacked the stunned warlord.

Boarhammer found himself up against the balcony, the railing creaking as his weight fell against it. Trick's hand shot out and he grabbed the black moon pendant from the warlord's flailing grasp.

'That's mine, you murderous son of a –'

The insult never left Trick's lips. The tower lurched again, tipping back the other way and saving Boarhammer's hide. Now Trick was stumbling towards the yawning chasm, losing his footing and snatching at the splintered floorboards. The initiative was with the Lord of Sea Forge, who spied the dropped sword skittering about on the floor. His eyebrows arched, as he seemed to recognize it for the first time. Bending unsteadily, he picked up the sword.

'Ravenblade?' he whispered, his eyes shining through the red mask of his bloodied, battered face. His nephew returned to his side now the fighting was almost over, keen to be with his uncle as he struck the killing blow.

'Today is a good day, Hugo! I will be Boneshaker's right hand! I will be greater than Tombstone in the Dark Lord's eyes!'

His laughter grew to a chuckling crescendo, a gurgle of phlegm and blood in his bloated throat as his victory was realized. The boy joined him, his shrill laughter even more disturbing than his uncle's. Boarhammer's white teeth formed a crescent moon of their own as he grinned, raising the blade to strike Trick.

Trick hung on to the broken floor, his mother's pendant clenched in his fist, stifling a sob as he prepared for the worst. Then, beyond Boarhammer, he saw a huge dark shape leap up from the arena, rising beyond the balcony, a great dark blob of warty flesh. A white-haired, blue-skinned warrior straddled it, his bare feet striking the giant toad behind the jaws.

The monster's mouth opened, and a long, sticky tongue shot out, covering six metres to strike Boarhammer in the back. The glob of mucus-drenched muscle took hold of the warlord, as surely as if he were a bug for lunch. The Lord of Sea Forge dropped Ravenblade and uttered a single squeal before the tongue retracted, ripping him off the tower top as the toad swallowed him in a great, greedy gulp. Then the blond boy was screaming, staggering, teetering on the edge of the jagged, smoking chasm.

The tower fell – splitting, breaking and roaring, flames licking around Trick as the world gave way beneath them.

# CHAPTER THIRTY-FOUR

The jolts in his pocket were what stirred Trick back to consciousness; Sparky the lightning bug was releasing a sudden, sharp charge. Trick's eyes blinked open as he stared up at the dirty sky. A trio of vultures circled overhead, black and menacing against the smoke-choked heavens, their squawks drifting down on the breeze. His throat was dry, the smell and taste of blood and soot a thick and heady mix.

'You're awake.'

It was Erika. Trick turned his head where he lay on the ground. He was on a clifftop, high above the docks of Sea Forge, the Lower City sprawling out below him. The Shield Maiden stood watching over him, her back to the arena, which still smouldered, poisoning the horizon with filthy clouds.

'How did I get out here?' Trick asked, struggling to

sit up as he gestured to the arena behind her. 'Last I remember, I was in there. Where's Kuro? How are the others?'

'He's on his feet. The ninja is mighty resilient. As are you, Trick Hope. You're tougher than you look.'

Trick managed a grim smile, even though his insides were screaming. Every sinew ached; his ribcage groaned and threatened to collapse at any moment.

'Boarhammer's tower. It came down, on fire. I don't remember what happened . . .'

'You were thrown clear as it toppled. Being on the balcony – or what was left of it – probably saved your life. Lucky I was in the arena to cushion your landing.'

'I landed on you?'

She laughed. 'I caught you. What? You thought I'd let you break your neck after all you'd done? Our friends were on hand to drag you and Kuro to safety.'

'Our friends?' It was coming back to Trick now, the fight on top of the balcony. With sickening dread he recalled the horrors that had befallen Kazumi and Toki. 'Zuma? Mungo?'

'Both alive, thank Odin.'

'Where are they?'

'They're with Kuro in the arena's ruins, searching the wreckage.'

She didn't need to say any more. Trick knew full well who they were looking for.

A noise overhead made them both look up. Kaw

landed in the branches of a nearby tree, ruffling his oily black feathers.

'Yeesh, those vultures take some seeing off, I tell ya. Typical of them to turn up when there's a free meal.'

Trick heard what the crow was saying. The arena was no doubt still littered with the bodies of the dead, good men and bad.

'You're a carrion crow, Kaw. Reckon you're showing great restraint not joining them.'

The bird shivered. 'Won't catch *me* feeding on the dead, pal. I got more style than that. Anyway, you done sleeping?' Kaw flapped down on to Erika's shoulder. 'You can't be lying about. Get a wiggle on – there's work to be done.'

'Wait, Kaw,' said Trick, drawing himself upright. Erika moved to help him but he raised a hand to ward her off. 'I'm not dancing to your tune until you've answered some questions.'

The crow looked back. 'It's the boss man, Kalaban, you really need to speak to, but I'll tell you what I can. At least let us walk and talk, flap and chat. Every moment's delay allows our enemies to regain the initiative.'

Trick picked up his gear from the ground and followed Erika and Kaw back towards the arena. The great gates that marked the entrance to the coliseum hung from their hinges, the wrought iron twisted and broken where they'd been forced from their brackets. The paved road that led through it was cracked and shattered, littered with debris and spattered with blood. The horrors of the arena had clearly spilled out into the streets of the Upper City. People passed them by, familiar-looking thieves and weary civilians, carrying the injured and the dead from the ruined site.

'Boarhammer's men have been routed?' asked Trick.

'Most of them have been sent packing,' replied Kaw.

'But some of our enemies are still near?'

'Oh, always,' squawked Kaw. 'Boarhammer's mob might've been turned out of Sea Forge, but the Wildlands are still riddled with the Skull Army. That's one warlord you've knocked off his perch, but there are others out there, and many more who'd take his place. Once Boneshaker gets wind of what happened here, you can be sure he'll be sending more nutters this way.'

'You should be gone by then, Trick,' added Erika. 'The men and women of Sea Forge can fight that battle themselves. You must visit other places that are in thrall to the Skull Army. Break Boneshaker's hold on the Wildlands as you build an army of your own that can defeat his minions.'

As they returned to the sand of the arena, the sun suddenly blazed down upon the three of them, the rays finding their way through the smoky air. The carcasses of slain monsters had attracted all kinds of carrion feeders, and crows and buzzards took flight from their feast as Trick and his friends passed by. Rescuers stopped what they were doing, waving Trick's way, some calling his name. The boy looked away, uncomfortable with the acknowledgement of strangers.

'Who said I wanted to build an army?'

'If you want to return to your home, it is the only way. You have to fight your way out of this world, Trick. There's no easy path, no simple shortcut.'

'I still say Kalaban should build this army. He was a great warrior once, wasn't he? He fought Boneshaker before. He can do it again.'

'Kalaban would gladly fight the Lord of Darkness again, but only when the time is right. We are but a handful right now, Trick,' Kaw said as they stepped between smouldering ash piles and tumbledown walls. 'You need to rebuild your group. Two of your friends were lost here, and your spirit was no doubt bruised by this battle.'

'Bruised but not broken,' chimed in Erika.

'People will follow Kalaban, though,' said Trick, the weight of expectation heavy and uncomfortable across his shoulders. 'This is his fight, not mine.'

'It's the fight of anyone with a good heart, child,' said Kaw, his voice softening now, becoming less harsh. 'We all must rise against our oppressors and make a stand, each of us however we can, in a bold or a small way. What I ask of you is huge, Trick. But, trust me, when the time is right, when you've rallied a force and we're closing on Boneshaker, I will reveal myself.'

'And you'll take him down?' asked Trick hopefully, realizing he was no longer talking to the crow.

'Alas, no, my young friend. It will be the Chosen One who defeats Boneshaker, nobody else. And, if *you* are defeated, Boneshaker will ultimately triumph. But I can help you, Trick. I will be your shield when the final fight begins. I'll draw his attacks and all his fury – let him think the battle is with me – while you strike the killing blow. Until then, it would cost us everything if the Lord of Darkness were to discover me alive. He would focus every godless soul in thrall to him upon me, and crush us all before we'd even struck a blow against him. You must be our champion, the Black Moon Warrior that the free people can rally behind.'

Trick looked at Kaw. The crow's talons were gripped tight to Erika's shoulder, his body frozen like a statue. The black bird's eyes were white, as the voice of Kalaban came through loud and clear.

'I've said it before,' said Trick. 'I ain't a warrior.'

Erika stopped beside an enormous pile of scorched, smoking wood, where the sand beneath their feet was damp with water. It looked like the kind of enormous bonfire Trick might have seen back home in November, the only thing missing being a sky full of fireworks. The inferno had now been doused, and rescue parties worked hard to stop the fire spreading.

Erika squeezed Trick's hands and looked hard at the boy. 'You took up the blade, Trick. When you had to, you wielded Ravenblade, and you smote Boarhammer. The warlord was one of Boneshaker's favourites, his attack dog. And you, *Trick Hope*, beat him down.'

'Hardly. I was just defending myself. He would have killed me if Mungo hadn't jumped in.'

'And that is our challenge, Trick,' replied Kalaban through Kaw's snapping beak. 'We need to surround you with warriors. Men and women who will fight for you. Bleed for you. Die for you, if they must.'

Trick looked around. Among the many ordinary people who had set to work rescuing the injured from the wreckage of the arena he spied warriors, men and women alike. He'd seen them before, in the arena, as the madness was about to erupt. They watched him with hard faces and cold eyes. Crixus was among them, the drunken gladiator who'd played his part in the Broken Shield brawl. He nodded at Trick. Were they judging him? Weighing him up?

Right on cue there was a commotion beside the giant pile of smoking timbers, as a trio of people made their way through the debris. All three warriors were covered in soot and sweat, heads bowed and wearied from their exhausting work. Mungo and Zuma came first, the Celt and the Aztec carrying the body of a red-headed youth between them. Kuro came last, limping along solemnly at the rear. Trick staggered closer as the men laid their comrade down upon the sand of the arena.

'Kazumi?' whispered Erika as Trick rushed to his friend's side. The men shook their heads.

'No sign,' said Zuma.

'I'll keep looking,' said Kuro. 'No warrior should be left behind, especially one so brave as the samurai.'

'Wake up, sleepyhead,' said Trick, kneeling to brush a curl of wiry hair from Toki's pale face. The others gathered round him, all joining him on their knees in a circle. Toki's eyes fluttered open, the effort taking all his strength. His painful smile revealed teeth stained red with blood. Trick fought back the tears as Toki spoke.

'What an adventure we've had, Trick Hope,' he managed to say, each breath a battle.

'And we'll have more, Toki,' said Trick, taking his friend's limp hand in his own and lifting it to his face. 'Don't be bailing on me, mate.'

Toki looked past Trick to Erika. 'Shield Maiden. You have found her. Take good care of Trick. He is a good man.'

'Valhalla awaits you, Toki,' said Erika stiffly at Trick's shoulder. 'You will be prepared for that journey as befits the greatest Viking warrior. I make you this promise also: I shall protect your friend, as you did before me.'

'He isn't my friend,' whispered Toki, every word a struggle. He made a fist as he took his dying breath. 'He's my brother.'

The hand fell against the young Viking's breast, lifeless. Trick nodded, unable to hold back the tears.

Toki hadn't been much older than him. Indeed, he was the closest to him in age of any of the warriors. And he'd been a friend to him. A brother. Trick curled his fingers and reached out. His arm shook, knuckles trembling with emotion as they glanced against Toki's limp hand. Blue-painted fingers reached out and held Trick's forearm, steadying it in a firm, fierce grip. He looked up at Mungo, and saw that the wild Celt's often crazed face was strangely calm and peaceful. Letting go of Trick's forearm, he held his fist against Trick's.

'Brother,' said Mungo, as one after another the surviving warriors each placed their fist against Trick's and repeated the word.

'Brother,' they all repeated together, their fists joined, arms forming the spokes of a wheel of warriors. More warriors and civilians gathered round them, joining the heroes and paying their respects to their fallen comrade. Kaw flapped his wings, ruffling his feathers. From a great distance away, in a cave behind a waterfall, the hermit watched them. He nodded. He wept. And he smiled.

# CHAPTER THIRTY-FIVE

It was dusk, and thousands had gathered in Sea Forge, lining the dock-front doorways, windows and rooftops. A flotilla of boats bobbed in the choppy water, each filled with mourners here to pay their respects. The grisly gallows and gibbets that had lined the harbour front had been torn down and all signs of Boarhammer's reign removed from sight.

The gates that had barred the way to the Upper City via the cliff road were open, for now at least. Never again would the poor be kept down. Whatever wealth was to be made in Sea Forge would be shared out henceforth. The gates would remain open, at least until the Skull Army returned. That would happen, no doubt, and the people of the city port would be prepared.

Impressive though the crowd was, Trick felt cold and alone. Across the water, drifting on the tide, was the riverboat, loaded with a pyre of wood and straw. Toki lay upon it, hands closed round the hilt of the sword that rested upon his chest. This was Toki's final journey, to who knew where? Trick wasn't religious; he had no idea what was out there when you died, if anything. Maybe there was a Valhalla for the Viking, where his forefathers would be waiting for him to drink mead and feast. Or perhaps he would find himself transported back to his own world and time. It wasn't a theory Trick fancied testing. He shivered at the thought.

Mungo, Kuro and Zuma surrounded him, while Erika stood apart from them. They were at the end of the long stone jetty that reached out into the harbour. She held a bow and arrow, the missile's tip coated in oily rags. Kuro stepped forward, a burning brand in hand, as Erika brushed the arrowhead against the flame.

The fire blazed immediately, devouring the fuel-soaked wrappings. She brought the arrow back, black feathers bristling against her cheek as she took aim. Then the arrow was flying, arcing gracefully through the air before finding its mark across the water. The flames quickly spread, feeding upon the packed hay on the boat as the funeral pyre caught light. Erika dropped her head and lowered the bow solemnly as the vessel quickly became an inferno, dark clouds belching into the twilight sky.

The Shield Maiden stepped back to them, and Trick couldn't resist placing a sympathetic hand upon her shoulder. She looked up, her blue eyes intense. No tears on show, just anger.

'There will be a reckoning, friend,' she said coldly. 'My countryman fought for you, treated you as his brother. I take on his oath in Odin's name. My sword and shield are yours, Trick Hope, and vengeance shall be mine.'

In that moment Trick caught a glimpse of just how hard the Viking was, hewn from Nordic rock and carving her own legend upon any world she walked in. She handed the bow past Trick to Zuma.

'My thanks, Aztec,' she said, as Zuma nodded. He slung the bow over his shoulder where it rested against a quiver loaded with black-feathered arrows. Trick's mind instantly returned to the arena and Kazumi's awful end. He then spied Boarhammer's golden mace swinging from Zuma's hip. It figured; Zuma was there for the gold.

Kaw perched nearby on a ship's mast, surrounded by a group of irritated-looking gulls. The crow squawked at them, shooing them off as he flexed his black claws on the sail top. The crow would be coming with them. He would be their eyes and ears on the open road, and their way of reaching Kalaban should the need arise.

'Your boat is prepared,' said Kuro quietly, leading the heroes through the crowd on the pier. Trick limped along beside him, still battered after the fighting in the arena. His quarterstaff was gone, and had been replaced by Kazumi's broken naginata. The blade had been lost from the head, and the black wood now made the perfect replacement weapon. Still, Ravenblade hung from his hip, the black-beaked handle brushing Trick's belly.

Many whispered blessings as Trick and his companions passed by, some going so far as reaching out to touch them for luck. Gifts were handed to the heroes and Mungo was keen to accept anything that was edible. These brave warriors had defeated Boarhammer and broken his stranglehold on Sea Forge. Who knew what dangers awaited them ahead?

'Lord Hope,' said a man with dark hair, brushing his hand over Trick's shoulder to attract his attention.

Trick smiled awkwardly. 'I'm no lord,' he replied, but the man was not listening. He ushered a child from behind him, prompting her to move forward. She could only have been five years of age, and Trick recognized her. She was the girl from Warriors Landing, who he'd last seen in the arena. In her hands she held a bouquet of wild flowers which she held up to him. Trick's heart ached as he saw the tears that raced down her dirty cheeks – tears of happiness. He knelt and hugged her – briefly – but was overwhelmed by emotion. Taking the tiny bunch of flowers he stood, sniffing back his own tears. He mouthed the words *thank you* to the girl and was on his way again, the ninja still at his side.

'You'll head upriver under cover of darkness,' whispered Kuro. 'The roads will be watched, within and outside the city. Our enemies are everywhere, remember. Take the people's thanks now, then we'll get you off the streets and down into the sewers. The Thieves' Guild will send you on your way before anyone knows you've gone.'

'You're definitely not coming?' asked Trick.

'No,' said the ninja. 'There's too much to be done here. With Gorgo and Boarhammer both dead, there's a power vacuum in Sea Forge.'

'You mean to take the city for yourself?' asked Zuma, suspicion evident in his voice.

'Gods, no. I would help find the right man or woman for that task while maintaining some kind of order. Many in the Thieves' Guild look to me for guidance. I shall do what I can in the short term. Many villains linger within this city's walls, looking for advantage.'

'Your loyalty is admirable,' said Erika.

'You'll join us once things are sorted?' asked Trick.

'Perhaps,' said Kuro. 'Only my work in the arena ruins is not yet over. Kazumi is up there, somewhere, lost within the wreckage. I mean to find her, bury her as she deserves. Only then can I return and join you on your quest, Trick Hope.'

Kuro raised a black-gloved fist. Trick gave the now-obligatory bump and smiled. 'Be great to get you back aboard as soon as, mate. I hope you find her.'

'As do we all,' added Erika as they passed through the throng.

Trick managed to smile as he saw Mungo laden with foodstuffs: ham hocks, fresh bread and strings of sausages hanging round his neck. A plump chicken squawked in the crook of his arm, destined for the Celt's belly.

'Mungo eat,' said the blue-woad warrior, grinning at Trick cheerily. If anyone could keep the boy's spirit up, it was the crazy bearded berserker.

Trick caught sight of Zuma standing toe to toe with a familiar figure: Crixus.

'Is there a problem?' asked Trick, approaching the two of them.

'Says he'd like to join us,' replied the Aztec, eyes narrow as he studied the Roman.

'Is that right?' said Trick.

'Yours is a worthy cause, master,' replied the gladiator. 'You can add my trident to your arsenal.'

'I'm not sure we need it,' said Zuma, barely disguising his sneer. 'If you hadn't caused a ruckus in the Broken Shield, Toki may never have –'

'I'm honoured that you'd ask to join us, mate,' said Trick, cutting the Jaguar Warrior's rant short. 'Let me speak with my companions first.'

With that he turned away. He didn't have the energy to referee the bickering of these warriors, not this evening, after what they'd just been through. He spied the burning boat drifting out of the bay, towards the Sea of Night, its fiery reflection dancing crazily upon the waves.

His hand drifted over the raven-headed pommel of the obsidian sword on his hip. He hadn't wanted the weapon, had fought his destiny tooth and nail, but somehow Ravenblade had found her way into his hand. It seemed he was on a path now, one that was impossible to turn away from. He was surrounded by strangers but felt truly alone. When he spoke, the words were a whisper, heard by nobody but destined for his friend on his way to Valhalla.

'Laters, brother,' said Trick, punching his breast as he saluted the departed Viking. Kalaban's words returned. The hermit had been right about these warriors. Each had taught Trick a different lesson: Toki, loyalty; Kazumi, staff skills; Kuro, atonement. Practical or philosophical, it didn't matter. Each of his friends had gifted Trick something wonderful. He would never forget them. When he turned round, he found Erika waiting. 'Just the person.'

'I am?' she asked as Trick unbuckled the weapon belt from round his waist. He handed it to the Shield Maiden.

'You jest, surely? You would give me Ravenblade?'

'Please. Take it. Take her. It's not for me. Use it against our enemies. You know how. I don't; I never will.' He struck the naginata staff on the floor at his feet. 'Besides, I've got this. Don't need no stinking sword.'

Erika snapped the belt in place and grinned. 'Come, Trick Hope. We go nowhere without you.'

'I wish you would,' sighed the boy, managing a sly smile. She clapped his back and hugged him.

'But you'd miss all the fun!'

'This is *fun*?' Trick's words were incredulous and high-pitched, his breaking voice treacherous before the striking, blonde-haired warrior woman.

'Of course,' she said, her voice lacking irony, or humour or playfulness. Trick realized then that the Viking never joked. Erika simply didn't do funny.

'This battle may be won,' said the Shield Maiden, her voice cold as ice, 'but our war has just begun.'

# EPILOGUE

The covered wagon trundled along, its wheels bouncing off every rock and rut that pitted the road out of Sea Forge. On either side of the vehicle, a handful of Blackguard rode on war horses, the few surviving elite warriors of the slain warlord. The soldiers of the Skull Army trudged behind them, heads bowed, battered and beaten by the assault upon their city. This was no orderly march. They were a ragtag shambles of a fighting troop, weary and washed out.

The nobles and merchants who had been loyal to Boarhammer followed, in a caravan of carts and wagons loaded down with all their worldly belongings. These people had worked hard for their riches. They'd be damned if they'd leave them behind for the thieves who had taken their city from them.

Within the confines of the covered wagon, an old

woman sat cross-legged beside a body. A brass censer swung overhead, its heady smoke filling the cramped confines of the wagon. A carpet bag lay open beside her, a host of ugly-looking tools rattling around inside it. She reached a bony hand within, removing a sharpened flint dagger. Raising it high, she muttered a series of arcane words, her blind eyes rolling in their sockets until only the whites showed. Her familiar, a fat black rat, sat upon the chest of the body, ignoring its mistress as it nibbled at the lifeless figure's bandages. Its yellow incisors dug in, tugging at the blood-soaked cloths, trying to worry them loose to reach the burnt flesh beneath. The fire had consumed him. The fire had taken him.

The witch's eyes remained pale and milky as she drew the flint over her palm, opening the thin skin in a bloody line. Her incoherent burbling continued, frantic words that grew in speed and volume, her grey lips bumping as her ritual reached its climax. Her hand dropped, landing over the body's bandaged face as she cried out, shaking her free fist at the heavens. Her bloodied fingers clenched the wrapped head, the skull trembling beneath as fresh smoke suddenly billowed from the gore-stained muslin.

With ferocious speed, the body's hands shot up, one striking the witch's fingers from his face, the other seizing the rat. Hard. There was a crunching of brittle bones as the rodent died in his burnt grasp. The old woman gasped, sensing the death of her familiar in that awful instant. Then the fingers were clawing at the face, tearing the wrappings away from the blackened, splitting lips.

'Lord Hugo,' said the witch, sobbing at the loss of her familiar. 'You are returned to us. Praise be to the old one!'

The reed-thin voice came out loud and clear, all that remained of the blond-haired boy.

'Hugo . . . is dead. I am reborn in the flames. Call me . . . Inferno.'

The witch mouthed the name silently, felt the heat roll off the boy in terrible waves. An unnatural, blood-curdling heat.

'Take me . . . to Boneshaker,' said the mummified nephew of Boarhammer, his voice cracking along with his frazzled flesh. 'I have news of the Black Moon Warrior.'

# Can you decode the runes and find the ten character names hidden below?

If you look closely, you may find an eleventh name for a clue about book two!

_____  _____  _____

# WORLD OF WARRIORS

## OFFICIAL GUIDE

## CRAFT TALISMANS!
## TRAIN WARRIORS!
## RNESS ELEMENTAL POWER

YOURSELF WITH ALL THESE SKILLS AND MORE,
OUR BATTLE AGAINST THE DEADLY SKULL ARMY

# WORLD OF WARRIORS

# W

## BOOK OF WARRIORS

# WORLD OF WARRIORS

## OFFICIAL STICKER BOOK

**OVER 1000 STICKERS!**

**USE YOUR STICKERS TO WIN DUELS,
COMPLETE ACTIVITIES
AND BUILD YOUR OWN ARMIES!**

# ABOUT THE AUTHOR

The designer of *Bob the Builder*, creator of *Frankenstein's Cat* and *Raa Raa the Noisy Lion*, and the author/illustrator of numerous children's books, Curtis Jobling lives with his family in Cheshire, England.

**CURTIS JOBLING**

Early work on Aardman's *Wallace & Gromit* and Tim Burton's *Mars Attacks* led to him picking up his crayons in 1997 to design the BAFTA-winning Bob. The animated series of *Frankenstein's Cat*, based on Curtis's book of the same name, picked up the Pulcinella award for Best Children's Show at the 2008 International Cartoons On The Bay festival in Salerno, Italy. His noisy new pre-school show, *Raa Raa the Noisy Lion*, can be seen on CBeebies, while his original paintings and prints sell in galleries the world over.

Although well known for his work in TV and picture books, Curtis's other love has always been horror and fantasy for an older audience. The Wereworld series of acclaimed middle-grade novels was published internationally by Penguin, with the first book, *Rise of the Wolf*, being shortlisted for the Waterstones Book Prize. The first of his Haunt novels for young adults was published in 2014, while 2015 will see the worldwide launch of *The Thirteenth Curse*, the first in Curtis's new Max Helsing series.

**Follow Curtis on Twitter @CurtisJobling**

# ~TOKI~

## THE VIKING WARRIOR

Famed for his heroism and swordsmanship, Toki was summoned to the Wildlands as he leapt from his blazing longship during a calamitous dawn raid. But all that seems like a distant memory now, and if it weren't for the scorch marks on his shield Toki would be certain he dreamt it.

**Summoned in:** AD 787
**Weapon:** Long sword
**Likes:** Thinking of home
**Dislikes:** Injustice
**Fighting fact:** Vikings settled arguments via ordeals: painful tests of bravery that included picking stones out of boiling water and carrying hunks of red-hot iron for nine paces.

# MUNGO

## THE CELTIC BERSERKER

Mad, blue and barbarous to know, Mungo is famed for his frenzied attacks on Roman settlements. But one thing this crazed Celt hates more than Romans is the fact he was summoned to the Wildlands while riding a war elephant across the Alps, alongside his hero Hannibal.

**Summoned in:** 218 BC
**Weapon:** Long sword
**Likes:** Rampant violence
**Dislikes:** Romans
**Fighting fact:** Celtic warriors often served as mercenaries and painted themselves blue to terrify enemies. Some even spiked and lime-washed their hair before battle.

# KAZUMI

## THE SAMURAI BRIDE

Legendary samurai Kazumi was summoned to the Wildlands as the Battle of Awazu raged around her. Having decapitated several enemies, she was taking cover behind a fallen horse when she felt a strange sensation. Now, desperate to re-engage the enemy, she lashes out at everyone she encounters.

**Summoned in:** AD 1184

**Weapon:** Naginata

**Likes:** Archery

**Dislikes:** Eels

**Fighting fact:** At up to eight feet long, the naginata gave female samurai a big reach advantage, and was ideal for planting in the ground to rip apart oncoming horses.

# -ZUMA-

## THE JAGUAR WARRIOR

Before entering the Wildlands, Zuma enraged fellow jaguar warriors with his reckless use of poisoned arrows. But they came in handy when he stumbled across a group of conquistadors carrying a hoard of stolen Aztec gold. The conquistadors are now mangrove mulch, but the gold was never found.

**Summoned in:** AD 1519

**Weapon:** Macuahuitl

**Likes:** Human sacrifice

**Dislikes:** Conquistadors

**Fighting fact:** As well as human sacrifice and gladiatorial combat, the Aztecs loved their macuahuitls – flesh-tearing wooden clubs embedded with razor-sharp chunks of obsidian.

# - KURO -

## THE MIDNIGHT NINJA

Master of stealth, Kuro has refused to remove his black garb ever since he arrived in the Wildlands. This has led to rumours that he is the mysterious ninja warrior who was last spotted scaling Azuchi Castle shortly before an assassination attempt on a notorious Japanese warlord.

**Summoned in:** AD 1579

**Weapon:** Chokuto

**Likes:** Espionage

**Dislikes:** Loud noises

**Fighting fact:** Ninja sometimes used blowguns (fukiya) to temporarily disable targets with blinding powder made from crushed glass, pepper and iron filings.

# -ERIKA-

## The Viking Shield Maiden

With her fiery temper, it's no surprise Erika was summoned to the Wildlands while wreaking blood-spattered mayhem. But she was wreaking it against her Viking shipmates after they mocked her for showing a kidnapped priest mercy, gutting the lot of them before they had even finished laughing!

**Summoned in:** AD 621
**Weapon:** Long sword
**Likes:** Invading foreign lands
**Dislikes:** Being laughed at
**Fighting fact:** Viking axes were capable of cutting through iron helmets and splicing down through the skull, coming to rest near the teeth! Now that's gotta hurt!

## Did you find them all?
## Well done, warrior!

And how about that eleventh name? It's **THE GATEKEEPER**
– look out for him in book two . . .

 # Listen

## Do you love
## listening to stories?

## Want to know what happens
## behind the scenes in a
## recording studio?

Hear funny sound effects, exclusive
author interviews and the best books
read by famous authors and actors
on the **Puffin Podcast** at
**www.puffinbooks.com**

# #ListenWithPuffin